T0157945

THE FAVORITE

FRANKLYN C. THOMAS

iUniverse LLC
Bloomington

THE FAVORITE

iUniverse books may be ordered through booksellers or by contacting:

iUniverse
1663 Liberty Drive
Bloomington, IN 47403
www.iuniverse.com
1-800-Authors (1-800-288-4677)

Because of the dynamic nature of the Internet, any web addresses or links contained in this book may have changed since publication and may no longer be valid. The views expressed in this work are solely those of the author and do not necessarily reflect the views of the publisher, and the publisher hereby disclaims any responsibility for them.

Any people depicted in stock imagery provided by Thinkstock are models, and such images are being used for illustrative purposes only. Certain stock imagery © Thinkstock.

ISBN: 978-1-4917-1901-5 (sc)
ISBN: 978-1-4917-1900-8 (hc)
ISBN: 978-1-4917-1899-5 (e)

Library of Congress Control Number: 2013923010

Printed in the United States of America.

iUniverse rev. date: 12/27/2013

For my family, who keeps me grounded.

Prologue

Last night…

The tapping of the smooth silver ballpoint pen against the notepad sounded like a metronome gone out of control. Crumpled balls of paper littered the handsome wooden desk, a graveyard of bad ideas growing larger as the pad of paper in front of him grew thinner. The paper's watermark – a green-tinged lion's head logo – stared at him, mocking him, daring him to try again to write something poignant. Or even just intelligent. In fact, at this point, the lion would even have settled for something merely coherent.

He reached for the tiny bottle of vodka from the mini-bar and emptied the last of the clear, caustic liquid down his throat. He felt his face flush as the liquor burned a path into his stomach.

He closed his eyes and enjoyed drifting off to drunkenness.

When his mouth and throat cooled he reopened his eyes. The lion still looked at him expectantly, waiting for him to begin this manifesto, this great work that would make her understand why. He tentatively put the pen to paper and scribbled out the letter's opening line.

To whom it may concern…

He had barely formed the final "n" when he tore the page from its pad. *To whom it may concern,* he thought. *Brilliant. Just brilliant.*

He tossed the balled up sheet of paper to the side and started again, dating the top of the page. He went over in his mind how letters were supposed to start, with Dear Someone, or Dearest Whomever. He wrote: *I don't even know your name.*

He smiled as he finished writing that one line. He cracked open another tiny bottle and sucked it down. He was drunker than he had been in a long time, but at least the words were flowing.

My name is Michael Dane. I'm your father. A little Darth Vader-esque, he thought, but it worked. *If you're reading this then I'm dead.* He paused a moment after he wrote that; the finality of those words made his stomach gurgle. Doubt, nervousness and fear crept into his mind for the first time since this crazy thing started. He wondered if this whole deal was such a good idea after all.

Drunkenness helped him rediscover his resolve. He had no choice after all. He wrote: *And of course you're reading this, because I know I'm going to die.*

Chapter One

T he lights in the locker room hummed and flickered above Michael Dane's head as the last of the gauze was taped tightly to his hands. He looked up and held his breath for a moment as he punched the palms of his hands, exhaling when the fluorescent rods snapped back on full strength, buzzing as if a fly were trapped inside. Soon after, they flickered again, and something in his stomach danced to the rhythm of the lights. When fully lit, the locker room was cream-colored brick from the ground up to about three feet, with drywall painted not quite white—beige, or maybe eggshell— going up to the ceiling. Michael sat on an elevated table in the center of the room, a small metal bowl with gauze, tape and scissors next to him. The table was brown leather and heavily padded, like the one he saw in his doctor's office. The lights dimmed again, freezing Michael's breath. He exhaled only when they came back on.

"Why don't they do something about that?" He flexed his wrists to test the support of the gauze. "It's annoying."

The pot-bellied black man in his early fifties putting the tape on Michael's hands stood from the stool in front of the table and admired his work. "Perfect," he said. "Let's get the gloves." He hustled over to a locker on the other side of the room and pulled out a pair of black boxing gloves with "DANE" printed on the wrists in gold block letters.

Michael took another deep breath to try to stop the salsa dancing girls in his stomach as the gloves were slid onto his hands. "This is it, Dutch," he said to the fat man as the gloves were tied up. "Showtime." He hopped off the table and rolled his neck from side to side, shadowboxing his way toward the wall, bobbing, weaving, and striking his imaginary opponent.

Terrence "Dutch" Masters glanced over Michael's shoulder at the clock on the wall. "Easy, killer," he laughed. "Don't tire yourself out. We still got at least ten minutes. Keep your shorts on." Michael laughed too and stopped shadowboxing. The dancing in his stomach changed from salsa to a waltz. Dutch tightened the laces on the gloves and looked up at his fighter. "God damn it," he said. "I can't believe we're finally here. Main event, title fight. It's been a long time coming."

"Relax," Michael said. "Everything's going to be fine."

"Be nice to get out there and get it over with. I'm too old for this stress."

Michael smiled quickly from the corner of his mouth. "Stop worrying," he said. "You trained me, didn't you? Haven't we been working to get right here, right now since I was like twelve? I'm ready, Dutch, don't stress it. I got a job to do." Michael flexed his hands through the tape and took a deep breath. Tension rippled through his arms as every muscle bulged and relaxed in succession. "You're making me nervous."

"You should be. Nervous is good. It keeps you focused, careful, and on your feet." Dutch wrapped duct tape around Michael's gloves at the wrists, then helped Michael get his silver robe on. "You ready?"

Michael nodded and bounced on the balls of his feet. "Born ready," he said as he led the way toward the ring, shadowboxing his way out the door. Dutch rolled his eyes at the statement and followed his fighter out.

One by one, people funneled into the MGM Grand Garden Arena in Las Vegas. The crowd grew steadily to capacity, and the people coming in late were hard pressed to make it to their seats. It was only a few minutes before the main event was scheduled to start: the IBF Light-Heavyweight Champion Quin Cortez vs. the well-regarded Michael Dane for twelve rounds. The excitement was palpable as the chatter intensified with the increasing crowd. Cortez, a lean, chiseled Dominican with a devastating right hook, had mowed down everything in his path to this point and his fights had been so short lately that his pay-per-view bouts were offered by the round. His supporters and detractors both agreed he had never been challenged, and there weren't very many in the division who could. Dane, on the other hand, was a veteran who insiders felt never quite reached his potential. Tough and strong, he usually finished fights with a powerful overhand right and was undefeated since his release from prison eighteen months before. While many felt he had lost his best years incarcerated for a gun violation Dane was the slight favorite, viewed as the first real fight Cortez would have since he won the title.

The rest of the card had just been a warm-up for this, but the early comers and die-hards wouldn't deny themselves an undercard fight, especially those who had paid for whole night. The fights themselves were exciting enough. One featured a couple of unknown middleweights from Mexico that went eight rounds before one of them was dropped by a surprise right hook. Another bout had a has-been from Miami, Florida fight a never-was from Vancouver, British Columbia. That fight went the distance and ended in a draw; both fighters were bruised and bloody afterwards and the crowd showed its appreciation. They were only filler though, appetizers for Dane vs. Cortez. The past few weeks, Cortez and Dane sniped at each other in the press, and officials had to separate them at the previous night's weigh-in just before fireworks really started. The entire crowd was chomping at the bit for this to finally get underway.

A slender, dark-skinned man in a white three-piece suit— with a charcoal gray shirt, skinny red necktie and shiny white leather shoes— sat cross-legged in one of the reserved luxury skyboxes, above the press boxes and high above the crowd with a lit cigar firmly cued between his first two fingers. He checked his gleaming platinum watch impatiently as he took a deep drag on the cigar. A thin, young usher, no more than twenty years old, led a pair of middle-aged white men to the seats behind him. The kid seated the two men and came back to the well-dressed man. "Sir," he said, clearing his throat, "you can't smoke that in here."

The well-dressed man exhaled thick gray smoke from his nose. "Pardon me, son?" he said, fixing his lazy, but somehow intimidating stare on the usher. "I didn't catch that."

The usher's hands fidgeted a bit. "There's no smoking in here." His voice cracked and he cleared his throat again. "You're going to have to put that out."

The well-dressed man reared back and let out a sound halfway between smoker's hack and laughter. "You can't be serious," he said, letting the cigar hang from the corner of his mouth. He took another drag and blew out a ring of smoke. "You do know who I am, right?"

The usher's arm trembled as he pointed to the NO SMOKING UNDER PENALTY OF LAW sign posted directly above them. "I'm sorry," he said. "I really am going to have to ask you to put that out."

The well-dressed man turned his head and stared into the usher's eyes as they darted everywhere to avoid the gaze. The man sucked in a couple of quick puffs as he reached inside his coat pocket. When the man pulled out a silvery, rectangular cigar case, the usher breathed a deep sigh and his shoulders relaxed.

The well-dressed man tapped the ash on the floor. With a low hiss, he extinguished the cigar against the case. "Satisfied?" he said.

"I'm sorry, Mr. Alexander," the usher said. "Just doing my job."

"You're welcome," the well-dressed man said under his breath as the usher scurried off. Once the kid was out of sight, he pulled another cigar from the case.

"Hope you have better control of your fighter than you do your event, Dante." The man in white looked around for the source of this statement and saw a Puerto Rican man in a black suit sitting behind him. He was young-looking, maybe thirty, and showed a row of perfectly aligned teeth as he smiled from ear to ear. He ran a hand through his impeccable hair and laughed. "I'd hate to think you have a hard time keeping everything in check. If that's the case he'll walk all over you." Dante reached into his jacket pocket for his lighter with his left hand, and flipped the Puerto Rican man off with his right. The Puerto Rican laughed again. "You have the money? Contract signed?"

"Trust me, Miguel," Dante said. He lit the cigar and took a quick drag. "Everything's set. You'll get paid after the fight. Just remember your end of the deal."

Miguel Castillo smiled and leaned back in his seat. "Don't worry about that. I'll deliver when you deliver."

"Then shut the hell up." Dante turned his attention toward the ring. "It's about to start."

✶   ✶   ✶

5

In the gray, dimly-lit hallway leading to the ring, Michael Dane bounced on the balls of his feet and pounded his gloves together as Dutch paced in front of the closed door. An official from the Athletics Commission inspected Michael's gloves for anything illegal. When he was satisfied, he signed the duct tape and waved them through.

Security guards in bright yellow blazers opened the door from the inside of the arena and motioned them in. Blinding white spotlights shone directly on the chiseled light-skinned black man with the shaved head and his portly, broad-shouldered, darker trainer. The roar of the crowd and the thumping bass line of Busta Rhymes' "We Could Take It Outside" poured through the open door as if being sucked out by a vacuum. Dutch put his hands on Michael's shoulders and pushed him out.

"It's show time," he said again as he walked behind his protégé.

Michael stalked toward the ring, close to the fans, as always, so they could touch him. He rolled his neck from side to side as he approached the ring. Flash bulbs and spotlights blinded him momentarily and every time his eyes adjusted, another would go off. Dutch walked behind him, keeping his hands on Michael's shoulders as they made their way through the crowd. They looked up at the giant video screen suspended above the ring and saw their high-definition reflection, twenty times life size. Michael climbed the ring steps at his corner, stepped between the ropes and raised a fist in the air. After Dutch took off his robe, Michael climbed the ropes in the corner, rubbed the panther's paw tattoo on his chest and pointed out to the crowd.

Chapter Two

Twelve weeks earlier…

Michael looked over at the Dante Alexander's massive, ursine bodyguard and pondered how he got himself into this situation. He was supposed to be training, in anticipation of a title fight. Now he was riding in a dimly lit four-by-six elevator that smelled like piss and whined as the ancient cable pulley inched the little box upwards. Instead of being surrounded by trainers, he was in the company of Jason Boone, a well-dressed six-foot-six, 350 pound black bear of a man, and the black bean burrito Boone kept belching up through this interminable ride. Boone wore a black suit, red shirt and black tie, as always. His shiny black shoes reflected what little light was in the elevator. Even though it was summer, he wore black leather driving gloves and even though he was indoors at night, he wore polarized sunglasses. He looked more like a businessman or a Detective than a bodyguard, and his bear-like face, complete with a thick beard, didn't even register a sweat in the stifling city heat.

"I got Boone doing something for me in the projects by Long Island City," Michael remembered Dante saying in his office earlier that day. "I need you to go with him. It's nothing major, there shouldn't be any trouble. I normally wouldn't ask you, but I got no one else."

Michael chuckled to himself. Of course, Dante wouldn't normally ask. Dante never actually *asked*. "What for, though?" Michael had replied. "Boone's a big boy, I'm sure he can handle himself."

Dante smiled. "This is true. It couldn't hurt to have an extra pair of hands though, right?"

Michael was relieved when the grimy and cramped little elevator finally creaked open at the twelfth floor. He wasn't sure that it ever actually would. Every slight movement made the elevator sway a bit and dimmed the lights, and there was just barely enough room in there for Michael, Boone and Boone's burrito halitosis. Boone walked out and Michael followed, letting out a deeply held breath.

"And of course, you'll be very well compensated for your time," Dante had said. Michael remembered the smile Dante was wearing: friendly on the surface, menacing about half a layer underneath. It was like a neighbor's dog about to warn you he was done playing. "Do you trust me?"

"On this? Not really."

Dante laughed. "I appreciate your honesty."

"I don't want to hurt anyone, Dante. I'm done with that part of my life."

"Michael," Dante said, "you're a prize fighter. You train yourself night and day in the art of hurting people. You get paid a lot of money to hurt people. It's not that big of a deal. Plus, how do you think we can afford your training?"

Michael closed his eyes and took a deep breath. "So what exactly are we doing?"

"Hey, wake up," Boone said as now they stood in front of Apartment 12C. "You ready?" Michael nodded, and Boone knocked on the reinforced steel door. After a few moments of silence, Boone knocked again.

"I'm coming, I'm coming," Michael heard faintly from inside the apartment, followed immediately by some shuffling, either of people or items. A tall, skinny black man pulled the door open as much as the security chain allowed and peeked out. His matted hair looked like it hadn't seen a comb in weeks, and an acrid smell seeped from his pores. He nervously looked to his left and saw Boone. "Who are you?"

"Dante sent me," he said. "Are you Ray-Ray?"

Ray-Ray looked to the right side of the door and saw Michael. "Who's this?"

Michael looked at Boone from the corner of his eye, who took off his sunglasses and put them in his jacket pocket. "Extra pair of hands," Boone said.

Apartment 12C was nearly barren. The four people passed out on and around the couch in the living room space served as most of the dwelling's furniture. The one dim lamp in the center of the room and the dull blue static haze coming from the TV made up the room's lighting. Ray-Ray led them to a small round dining table by the window in that poorly lit living room. On the table was a Bunsen burner, the kind Michael used in chemistry class before he dropped out of high school, and a small spoon that looked like it used to be silver. About two-thirds of the spoon had been burned black, and the business end of it was rust-brown, scarred with flakes and heat blisters. Michael felt his heart implode; *Figures,* he thought. *This is a dope deal.*

"I ain't expect Dante to send someone so soon." Ray-Ray scratched at his neck and shifted his weight uneasily from side to side as his eyes darted around the room. "It's a mess in here. I'd have cleaned up a bit, or something if I knew."

Boone raised his hand and Ray-Ray's blithering stopped. "You got the money?" Boone asked.

Ray-Ray scampered across the apartment to the kitchen and reached under the sink. He pulled out a faded red coffee can and removed an envelope. He scurried back to the living room space and handed it to Boone. "All there," Ray-Ray said. "Down to the last dollar."

"I hope so." Boone removed a stack of hundred-dollar bills from the envelope and peeled them off one by one. "I'd hate to be you if it wasn't."

"Whoa man, what are you doing? You're gonna count that right in front of me? That's fucked up. Don't you trust me?"

Boone shot him an icy glare, and once again Ray-Ray was silenced. "Of course not, Ray-Ray. But if it's all here, what difference does *that* make?" Boone counted for what seemed like an hour on the first pass and then counted the stack twice more before he jumped to his feet and grabbed Ray-Ray's throat in one fluid motion. "Where's the rest, Ray?"

Oh hell, Michael thought.

✳ ✳ ✳

"Mm-hmm," Boone said calmly into his cell phone as he held the lower half of Ray-Ray's face in his death grip. Ray-Ray's scream was muffled by the huge leather-gloved paw that covered his mouth. Boone lifted the phone away from his face. "Shush," he said to Ray-Ray.

Michael's eyes jumped wide and his mouth dropped. This situation took a hard left turn into uncomfortable territory, and regretted being there in the first place. "Yo, Boone, let him down," he said after a moment. "What the fuck are—"

"Shut up," Boone said, calmly, lifting the phone from his face for a split second before returning to his conversation. "Mm-hmm. Okay. Got it. Thanks." He closed his cell phone and got right into Ray-Ray's face. "Well, Ray," he said, tightening his grip, "today may be your lucky day." He let Ray-Ray go with a shove and put his sunglasses back on. "As you can imagine, Dante's not very happy about the money being light."

"I'm sorry, man," Ray-Ray whimpered as he gasped for breath and massaged his jaw. "I didn't know it wasn't all there. I wouldn't do that to Dante. I swear, I didn't know."

Boone put his hands up to concede the protest. "Of course you didn't," he said. "Honest mistake. We understand that, don't we, Mike?"

Michael nodded nervously. "You're only human," he said. "It could have happened to anyone."

"Yeah," Ray-Ray said. "Everyone makes mistakes, right? I'm sorry."

Boone smiled. "Exactly. Dante knows you're sorry, and he'll even forgive you, provided you have something he needs."

"Anything," Ray-Ray instantly replied. "If he needs it and I got it, it's his, no problem."

"That's the kind of cooperation I like to see, Ray." Boone cleared his throat before continuing. "You have anything to drink in here?" Ray-Ray hastily filled a plastic cup with water and handed it to Boone, who downed it in one gulp. "He needs information, Ray," he continued. "Where's the rest of the money?"

"It was supposed to be there," Ray-Ray said. "We sold some smack to some Jamaicans and we were supposed to collect from them yesterday. I-I mean, you know how Jamaicans can be flaky with this shit. I sent those dudes to collect." He pointed over to the four men passed out in the living room. "I don't know what happened."

Boone laughed for a second and unbuttoned his suit jacket. "You know, I told Dante the same thing on the phone just now.

You heard me tell him that you sold it and were waiting for the payout. I did my best to defend you, to get him to let it go. He seems to be convinced otherwise." Boone reached into his jacket and swatted Ray-Ray in the face with the barrel of his gold-plated 9mm, knocking him to the ground. "He also said you were into him about fifty grand. Can't expect him to let that go. Don't be stupid, Ray. Where is it? Where's the money?"

"I don't fuckin' know!" Ray-Ray said. His eyes widened and he started to sweat.

Michael was frozen in place as Boone pointed the gun at Ray-Ray. "Either you're lying or you're an idiot," Boone said. "In any case, if you don't cough up the money, the drugs, or the Jamaicans, you're useless to Dante." He clicked off the safety catch. "And useless means dead."

"Yo, for real, I don't know!" Ray-Ray said. He was breathing heavily now, and tears started to leak from his tightly closed eyes. "I swear to God, I don't know nothin' about what happened!"

Boone pulled the slide back and took a step away. "Well, Ray," he said with a heavy sigh, "that sounds a whole lot like a problem."

Finally forcing himself to make a move, Michael slid between Boone and Ray-Ray and shoved Boone back. "Yo, man," Michael said, "are you crazy?"

Boone peeked around the end of his gun and smiled coolly at Michael. "I was just about to ask you the same thing."

Michael looked down at Ray-Ray, on the ground with his eyes shut tight, then at the killer end of Boone's gold-plated nine. His heartbeat grew louder as he felt it crawl up his throat. He tried his best to ignore the flight part of the fight or flight response.

Then again, he thought, *fighting probably isn't the best idea, either.*

"Get out of the way, Michael," Boone said calmly.

"What are you doing, man?" Michael asked, voice quavering. "Are you out of your mind?"

Boone smiled. "You're asking *me?* You're the one standing between the gun and the junkie."

Michael shook his head and took a step toward Boone. "Come on, big man, you know this isn't right. He don't have what you want. Put the gun down."

Boone reached into his jacket with his free hand and produced another gold-plated nine and pointed it at Michael. "Step aside," he said, though Michael could barely hear him over the sound of his heartbeat pulsing through his ears. "Please. I don't want to kill you."

Michael's body tensed and his fingers went numb. "Yo, what the fuck are you doing?"

"*Please,*" Boone said, louder and more assertive, cutting Michael off. "Move." Michael hesitantly stepped to his left and the barrel of Boone's gun followed him. "Now, as I was saying, Ray-Ray, I need to know where the Jamaicans are."

Ray-Ray's eyes were wide and glassy. He took, short shallow breaths as his eyes darted back and forth between Boone and Michael.

"Ray, wake up," Boone tapped the junkie with the side of his foot. "I asked you a question. Jamaicans. Where are they?"

"I don't know, man," Ray-Ray whined. "I swear."

Boone turned the second gun on the crying addict on the ground and Michael caught himself saying, "Oh thank God," involuntarily as his body relaxed.

"That's not the answer I needed to hear, Ray."

"It's the fucking truth, I swear to fucking God. I haven't seen or heard from them. I thought they was dead or got popped by the Five-O."

"Come on, Ray, stop fucking with me. If you don't have my money, my dope, or the information I need, why are we letting you live?" He flipped off the safety catch on the other gun and used his free fingers to pull the slide back. "You're useless."

"I'll get it!"

Boone paused. Michael was again frozen in place, and for a moment, the only sound in the room was Ray-Ray's panicked whimpering. "I'll get it," he said again. "Tell Dante I'll get it."

"Get what Ray?" Boone said. "What are you getting?"

"Information. On how to find those motherfuckers. They have Dante's money. I'll get it. J-just please, don't kill me." Ray-Ray's words turned into barely comprehensible sobs. "Just please don't kill me, please, please don't kill me."

Time in the living room slowed down. Michael's pounding heartbeat muted the other noises in the room—the white noise from the television, the hum from the halogen lamp, and the snores of the four men passed out on the couch. Boone's finger hovered over the trigger for a couple of moments before he flipped the safety catches of both guns back on. Ray-Ray let out a sigh of relief and a stream of urine in his pants as Boone put the guns back in his shoulder holsters. Boone looked over at the still shell-shocked Michael and nodded. He extended his hand to Ray-Ray and helped him to his feet. Ray-Ray shivered as Boone adjusted the man's tank top and mussed his matted hair. "Well, damn brother," he said in a calm whisper, "that's all you had to say."

☆ ☆ ☆

Boone drove along the Brooklyn-Queens Expressway on the way back, just above the 35 mile-per-hour speed limit. It was almost 10:00 p.m., and the highway quiet save for the normal Wednesday night New York activity. Boone drove straight and just fast enough to not slow up traffic. He turned on the smooth jazz station and drummed his fingers on the wheel, humming along to the wordless tune that came in over the radio, with no regard to the chaos that had just transpired.

Michael sat in the front passenger seat. He hadn't spoken a word since Boone drew a gun on him, but his heartbeat was returning to normal, finally. He took a deep breath and turned to Boone, who seemed relaxed—though with Boone's cool yet menacing exterior, Michael could never tell. At any rate, he didn't look like someone who had two men at gunpoint twenty minutes earlier.

Michael didn't realize he was staring until Boone cleared his throat and said, "I hope you don't think I'm cute."

Michael was jolted out of his daze. "What?"

"It's a miracle, you can speak," Boone said dryly. "I thought you went mute on me."

Michael rolled his eyes and looked out the passenger window. "Yeah. I'm fine. I'm all right, considering, you know, you had a gun pointed at me."

"Come on, now," Boone chuckled. "What that was back there was a classic case of 'good cop, bad cop.' It worked perfectly."

"You pulled. A gun. On me."

"Nothing personal, dog. Don't be mad."

"Nothing personal? I thought you were going to shoot me!"

Boone paused a moment and cocked his head to the side. "For a second, I *was*."

Michael's heart stopped for a beat and his eyes gaped.

"Oh relax," Boone said. "Stop being such a bitch, will you? It's not like I'd have *killed* you. I'd probably have gotten you in the arm or something. A flesh wound. I know you got the big fight coming up. You did the smart thing though, and got out of the way. You let the bad cop do his job."

Michael hissed through his teeth. "You're fucking crazy, you know that?"

"Like I said, it was nothing personal. It's just business."

Chapter Three

When his music stopped, and the lights in the arena went dark, Michael took a deep breath. He shook out his arms and legs and rolled his neck to get loose. Red, white, and blue strobe lights shone on the arena entrance directly opposite where Michael and Dutch had just entered. A 5-second countdown went up on the giant screen, and the fans started chanting along at 3.

They're eating this shit up, Michael thought.

The door opened and in came the champion, Quin Cortez, "El Conquistador." He strode forth to Bamboleo's "El Bueno Soy Yo," accompanied by a throng of trainers, handlers, hangers-on, and security adorned in yellow blazers, most of them screaming and hollering gibberish about their boy being the champ. Michael was transfixed by the music; he knew that song word for Spanish word. It was one of Selena's favorites.

Selena.

Michael shook it off. *Head in the game, Mike,* he thought to himself.

He felt Dutch's hand on his shoulder. "Guess this guy thinks he's somebody, huh?" Dutch said.

"This guy?" A slight smile creased Michael's face. "Like being undefeated is all that tough. Or beating seven guys in less than two minutes."

Dutch smiled as well. "Or never having a fight go longer than six rounds."

"Exactly. Piece of cake." Michael looked over at the Cortez procession as it made its way to the ring. Ten guys climbed through the ropes, last of them being the man himself, Quin Cortez, draped in the flag of the Dominican Republic. He looked taller than his 5-feet-10-inches somehow, using that flag as a robe. He paraded around the ring before stopping at Michael's corner, extending his arms to unfurl the flag behind him before he twirled and dropped it at Michael's feet. The capacity crowd roared at everything the champion did, and he had no shame in basking in their affection.

Michael looked down at the flag, and then eyed Cortez up and down. The champ was even dressed like a flag, with the half-silver, half-blue trunks, the red high-tops, and gloves with a single silver star on each. Brow furrowed and lips tightly pursed, the champion breathed heavily through his nose and stared at Michael with wide, unblinking eyes.

"What?" Michael said as the deafening crowd chanted "Quin Cor-tez! Quin Cor-tez!" The noise sounded like bacon crisping in a metal pan. "Am I supposed to be scared of you?"

Cortez smiled back, revealing perfectly aligned teeth – *probably all caps,* Michael thought – and took a step forward, kicking aside the flag. "You're done, son." Cortez mimed a throat-slash with his glove. "*Finito.* You ain't takin' this belt away from me."

Michael took a step forward, getting nose-to-nose with Cortez. "Try to stop me, chump." He trained his most intimidating glare on the champion's eyes. "I'm leaving with that belt. The only question is if you'll be awake to see it."

"Whatever. You gon' be my bitch just like everyone else."

As if to punctuate his fighter's bravado, Cortez's trainer forced his way between him and Michael and held the orange championship strap, pimped out with massive 24-karat gold plates, high above his head. Dutch got between Cortez's trainer and Michael, pushing his fighter back toward their corner.

"He got nothin'," Dutch said. "Don't let him get in your head! He got nothing for you except that belt! And after tonight, he won't even have that!"

Michael smiled slightly and laughed. "Thanks, old man. For everything."

"Let it Bang," the first single from the Hollowpointz's album, was on the radio in Boone's SUV as he and Michael drove up the West Side Highway. The track's opening bass line was met by Michael's bored groan. The Hollowpointz were the group that Dante produced and managed, and every time Michael went to see Dante, they were there, either physically or musically. Dante did his best to make the rap trio visible, and it was starting to pay dividends with heavy radio airplay. Michael changed the tuner to another hip-hop station. Boone pressed a button on the steering wheel and "Let it Bang" once again blared over the SUV's sound system. Michael hissed through his teeth and reached for the tuner again.

"Touch that radio again and I'll cut your hand off at the wrist."

Boone's threat froze Michael's hand and a disgusted look warped his face. "Oh come on," he said. "Are you serious? You've heard this song 10,000 times. You know these guys personally. You were in the studio when it was recorded. Aren't you a little sick of it by now?"

"That ain't the point." Boone said. He clicked the indicator and got off the highway at 125th Street. "I ain't ask you to change the station. This is *my* car. You don't sit in a man's car and change the station because you don't like the station, like it's all good and shit. *Especially* when you ain't driving. There's consequences for that."

Michael looked at the radio. "You telling me you *want* to hear this shit?"

"You know what the word 'passenger' means?" Boone asked as he took a hard stop at a red light at the intersection of 125th and Amsterdam that made Michael lurch forward in his seat. "It's ancient Egyptian for 'not the fucking driver,' so if you don't like it, get out and walk." Boone reached over and opened Michael's door as the light turned green. The traffic behind Boone honked impatiently as Michael fumed.

Michael rolled his eyes and closed the door. "Fine, goddamn it," he grumbled. "Keep the fucking song."

"Thank you," Boone said. "Passenger." He drove through the intersection as the light turned red again and promptly changed the radio to the other hip-hop station.

"This is such bullshit," Michael said. "I don't want to fucking be here. I told him, I don't like doing this shit. I ain't no thug. I should be in the ring, training right now, not in Washington Heights with a trigger-happy psychopath trying to track down some deadbeat Jamaican cat. I swear, if I wasn't so close to getting my title shot, I'd tell Dante to fuck off."

"We're here," Boone said, double-parking in front of a brown and red, six-story apartment building. Air-conditioning units stuck halfway out of propped-open windows, dripping condensation on the sidewalk below. Pieces of the building's façade, formerly ornate and reminiscent of a time when the neighborhood was new, were cracked and peeling paint dangled from spots like flesh from an open wound. Bags of trash lined the curb and had begun to rot in the unrelenting August heat and humidity.

"Wonderful," Michael said dryly. "This feels like a great way to spend the day."

Boone hit the emergency flashers and opened his door. "Stop whining and focus. We have work to do."

The six flight walk-up was a vast improvement in Michael's eyes to the cramped elevator from earlier, if for no other reason than not having his eyes tear up from Boone's breath. Otherwise the building was what could be expected for the neighborhood. The hallway lights flickered intermittently and shone dimly on the third and fourth floors. Garbage bags sat on every landing. Small piles of discarded cigar tobacco, left naked of the pungent paper that experienced blunt-rollers preferred, dusted the top and bottom stair of every flight. A visible haze lingered as they got closer to the roof, carrying with it the unmistakable scent of three-day-old "hydro." Business as usual for a building in this part of town.

Still, Michael thought, better the contact buzz than Boone's breath.

The weed smell was heaviest at the roof access, a black steel fire door that didn't latch tight. The "No Trespassing" sign and the alarm mechanism on the door was mostly for show; the alarms in these kinds of buildings never worked and provided little deterrent to those wanting to smoke weed on the roof. Boone waited at the door with his hand in his jacket pocket. "Remember," he whispered, "play your part, back me up, and don't do nothin' stupid."

"You're telling me to back you up like *I'm* the one who's strapped. The fuck am I, bulletproof?"

"Relax and stop bitchin'. These cats probably aren't packing anyway. Just go."

Probably, Michael thought as he clenched his teeth and took a deep breath.

Boone shook his head and reached into the holster on his ankle, under his left sock. He quickly unstrapped a semi-automatic .45 and handed it to Michael.

"Jesus," Michael said as he took the gun. "How many guns do you *carry?*" He made sure the safety was on and gripped the handle firmly. The textured steel was cold in his hand.

"On three."

Michael nodded and took a deep breath. He heard Boone click the safety catch off his gun.

"One."

Michael was surprised at how loose he was. He took another heavy breath and released the last bit of tension that had bunched in his shoulders.

"Two."

I hope I'm not getting used to this, Michael thought as he clicked off the safety latch. *Just keep focused on that title shot.*

"Three."

Boone kicked open the door and fired four shots in the air. Two Jamaican guys -- one tall and rail thin with a head full of dreadlocks tied in a ponytail, the other bald and short with a potbelly-- immediately dropped their weed, ducked low and scattered. Michael chased the bald one down and tackled him to the hot blacktop roof. He slammed the shiny, bare head on the ground twice and shoved the barrel of his gun against the base of the man's skull until he stopped resisting. When Michael looked up, he saw Boone put the other man in a chokehold and grab a fistful of his shoulder-length locks.

Boone put the barrel of his gun to the dread guy's temple and he promptly exchanged spirited struggle for quick, panicked breaths. "Good morning," Boone said. "Ray-Ray told us where to find you boys." The dread whimpered as the gold-plated 9mm pressed into his skull. "Good," Boone said. "Now nod if you know what this is about." He relaxed the chokehold enough for the dread to nod his head. "Good."

Boone dragged the dread to his feet and over to the steel ventilation shafts at the northeast corner of the roof. The steel shaft lazily emitted hot air from the incinerator in the building, and the shiny steel glinted in the bright summer sun. Boone sat him down on the vent, and as the dreadlocked man's skin started to cook through his clothes, Boone put the gun back on the Jamaican's dreadlocked skull. "I need some information," Boone said. "You've got three chances to give it to me. If we have to go past the third chance, you will probably be dead. Do you understand me?"

"Tell him what he wants to know," Michael said in his best "good cop" voice. "Don't let it come to that." The dread nodded and Michael was relieved.

"Ray-Ray told me you knew where my money was," Boone said. "Where is it?"

The dread paused for a moment; he shot a quick, nervous look at Michael before facing Boone. "I don' know what yuh ah chat 'bout," he said defiantly.

Boone glanced down at the roof, then reared back and swatted the dread across the mouth with the barrel of his gun. Michael winced as three teeth and a mouthful of blood spewed from the man's face. "That's strike one," Boone said. "I ask you again, where is my fifty grand?"

The dread coughed and spit up more blood. "I don' know," he gasped. "Ray-Ray disappear t'ree months ago. Mi' neva hear from 'im since."

Boone took a deep breath and cocked the slide back on his gun. "That would be strike two," he said coldly.

Michael's mouth hung open as Boone, in a flash, pressed the barrel of the gun into the dread's thigh, just above the knee and fired. While the explosion from the muzzle was muted by flesh and bone, the squishy sound of hot lead tearing through muscle and sinew, and the accompanying geyser of crimson, were seared into Michael's consciousness. The dread's bloodcurdling scream carried for blocks, and Michael couldn't help but turn and puke on the dread's partner.

"And that was just your knee," Boone said over the dread's sobs. With his free hand, Boone wiped blood splatter off his own brow. "There are a couple of possibilities here. Either you're lying, which would make you stupid, or you're not, which would make you very unlucky. Either way, unless you tell me what I need to know, your day will end badly."

"Boone," Michael wheezed after emptying the contents of his stomach. "Come on, man, back off. Don't do this."

"Which is it?" Boone demanded. "I don't like getting blood on my suit for no reason. Are you stupid or unlucky?"

"I don' know where it gone," the dread whined through a stream of tears. "I swear 'pon mi' muddah's grave, I don't know where the money gone!"

"Leave him alone, Boone," Michael said. "He doesn't know anything!"

Boone looked over at Michael briefly, then back at the dread, who was still writhing in pain and shock and trying not to scream. He pulled the slide on the gun back and ejected the spent shell, then pointed it back at the dread. "Unlucky then," Boone said before he fired three rounds into the dread's chest. He walked over toward Michael and fired four shots into the bald Jamaican lying prone on the ground, and holstered his weapon.

Michael stood up on the roof, horrified as the two men's blood flowed onto the asphalt. The smell of blood, incinerator exhaust and gunpowder overpowered him, and he turned toward the building's raised edge and dry-heaved. When he was done, he stumbled as his body shook uncontrollably and the loaded handgun rattled in his hand. Boone helped Michael to his feet and slipped the weapon out of his partner's shaking hands.

"We should probably go," he said, as he ushered Michael through the roof access door.

Chapter Four

Michael couldn't stop shaking.

He didn't know exactly how he got into Boone's car (Lord knows it was the last place he wanted to be) or when exactly it was that he stopped dry-heaving. The ringing in his ears had only just subsided, and the car seemed to wobble from the inside out. His stomach felt like a well-shaken soda can, and he couldn't figure out why his mouth was so dry. The one thing he knew for sure is that he had just witnessed a double homicide. Worse still, he participated. He was an accessory - or was it an enabler? - to a felony crime.

"Mike," Boone said. "You okay over there?" Boone didn't look terribly shaken up, but he was driving well over the speed limit. He narrowly avoided an accident as he ran a red light going down Broadway. The lights and cross-streets whizzed by Michael in a blur. "Mike, I need you to answer me. Are you okay?"

Michael's breathing quickened along with his pulse. Rushed, shallow breaths nearly matched his manic, adrenaline-fueled heart rate to the beat. His vision was blurry when he looked up at Boone, and he felt his palms get clammy. He felt his hands shaking and looked down at them; a sickly gray-ish pallor replaced Michael's normally healthy brown skin tone.

Franklyn C. Thomas

"Deep breaths, Mike," Boone said. Michael didn't find the instruction reassuring as Boone's SUV screamed down the wrong way on a one-way at 68th Street. "Come on, man, calm down. Don't get sick on the leather."

Michael took a deep, slow breath through his nose. The smell of the leather - hot from summer, wet from sweat and lightly fragrant with pine tree car fresheners - forced its way into his nose and threatened to make him upchuck again. He swallowed the urge, exhaled quickly and took another deep breath. "Oh, fuck," he exhaled, finally finding a high pitched, panicked voice. He took a slightly less deliberate breath and exhaled again slowly. "Oh, fuck. Oh fuck oh fuck oh fuck."

"Calm down, Mike," Boone repeated. His jaw tightened and he spoke through grit teeth. His tone remained even, but Michael could hear the agitation he was trying to hide. "There's nothing wrong, nothing to worry about."

"You shot them, you fucking psycho!" Michael shouted. "You shot them both, and you killed them right in front of me!"

"Relax, Mike, it's going to be okay."

"There are a couple of dead guys on that roof we just left. Tell me what part of that sounds okay?" Michael wiped the beads of sweat off his head. "You know what?" he panted. "You're fucking crazy. You and your boss are going to land me back at fucking Ryker's. I can't fuck with you people anymore. I'm done. You hear me? I'm out, I'm done, and it's over."

Boone's grip on the wheel tightened and he made sharp moves around traffic. A couple of consecutive hard turns sloshed Michael around the front seat. "Mike," he said through tightly gnashed teeth. "Shut the hell up and calm down already."

"Nah, man, you shut up. I'm gone. Let me out the car, man. I'm going home. I'm going home, and away from you and your psychotic ass!"

The tires screeched as Boone swerved to the side of the road, just before the 42nd Street entrance to the FDR, and put his hazard lights on. They were stopped for a bit when Michael looked over at him with his eyes wide open.

"Negro, is you stupid? Pulling us over by the side of the highway like that? You want the cops to --"

Michael was silenced by the sound of Boone pulling the slide back on his gun. He looked to his left and was eye to eye with the barrel of one of Boone's gold-plated 9mm's.

"Oh shit," Michael groaned. "You're gonna kill me too! I saw what you did and now you're gonna put two in *my* head and oh god I don't want to die please don't kill me I won't say nothing please --"

"Shut. The fuck. Up."

Michael held a deep breath, closed his eyes and tilted his head away from the gun. Sweat dripped from his face and his whole body shook violently. Boone kept the gun trained on Michael until he released the breath. He let out a breath of his own and clicked on the safety catch. He slowly holstered the gun and put his hands up.

"I'm not going to kill you," Boone said softly, letting out a deep, calming breath. "I'm not even going to hurt you. All I need is for you to calm down and listen to me."

Michael breathed slowly as Boone spoke, and felt his heart rate slow down from frantic to just excited.

"Are you good?" Boone asked and Michael nodded. "Good," he said. "Jesus, for someone who did a prison bid, you're really fucking jittery. Like you ain't never seen a dead body before."

"It was a weapons charge," Michael shouted. He took a couple of hurried breaths. "I'm not going back. "Not for you, not for Dante. Fuck that."

"Stop being so melodramatic. Dante will…"

"Dante will? Dante will what, Boone? Get us out of this? You killed a man."

"... Let us know what to do. He knew it might come to this. As a matter of fact, he gave me one last thing to do in case it did." Boone cruised down the FDR to the Tri-Borough Bridge, and in less than fifteen minutes, they found themselves in the same projects they were in the night before. Michael felt his stomach bubble intermittently during the ride and was grateful when the car finally stopped.

"Come on," Boone said. "We're going inside."

"I can't" Michael said, shaking his head. His face was sweaty and pale and he shook visibly in his seat. "I'm not going in there again. I'm not going anywhere with you."

Boone looked at his watch. "I'll be back in five minutes, then. If you leave the car, I'll find you and kill you. Not trying to get the ride stolen in the projects." Boone calmly strode away, and within a couple of minutes, Michael heard a pop. Then another, then three more in quick succession. Ray-Ray and his friends were very likely dead. As promised, five minutes later Boone returned to the vehicle, and without a word retraced his route out of the projects and back over the East River.

The ring announcer emerged from the crowd, stepped between the ropes and grabbed the microphone that dangled above the center of the ring. He cleared his throat and held the mic close. "And now, ladies and gentlemen, for tonight's main event - 12 rounds of boxing for the IBF World Light-Heavyweight Championship!" The crowd whooped and whistled as the ring girls took the championship belt from Cortez's trainer and paraded around the ring with it. The ring announcer motioned to the crowd to quiet down, and as the noise subsided he continued. "In the white corner, the Challenger; standing five feet, ten and one-quarter inches tall, weighing in at 171 and three-quarters pounds, fighting out of the Dewey Street Gym in Brooklyn, New York, wearing the black trunks with the gold trim, with a professional record of 22 wins and three losses with 19 wins by way of knockout…"

He paused to take a deep breath.

"'The Panther,' Michaaaaaaaael Daaaaaaaane!" Michael stepped toward the ropes and raised his fists, half the crowd chanting his name. He looked out to the crowd and imagined Dante Alexander, the event's promoter and booker, sitting just beyond the lights in the skybox, staring right back at him with a cigar dangling from between his fingers with a smug little knowing grin. Michael's arms tensed in anger. The fighter took a deep breath turned toward Dutch. He rolled his neck in a circle until he felt it crack, and he bounced on the balls of his feet.

"And in the red corner, standing five-feet-nine and weighing in at an even 170 pounds --" The ring announcer paused like he always did, succumbing to the crowd noise building for the champ, restarting his announcement once the crowd started chanting his name.

"Cortez! Cortez! Cortez!" Michael swore there must have been a speaker somewhere in the crowd rigged to start the chant.

"Hailing from Miami, Florida by way of Santo Domingo in the Dominican Republic, wearing the silver and blue trunks with a professional record of 20 wins and zero losses with 18 wins by knockout… he is the IBF Light-Heavyweight Champion of the Wooooorrrllld…"

Michael liked the way the ring announcer said that. Champion, emphasis on "champ." It had a sweet ring to it.

"'El Conquistadoorrr…'" He rolled the "r" for effect. "Quin Cortez!"

Cortez climbed the ropes in the corner, raised his hand toward the roof and pointed out to the crowd, holding the pose for the benefit of those with flash photography. As he hopped down from the ropes, his face went instantly from smiling for the crowd to scowling in the ring. Cortez's trainer, a Dominican man in his fifties who was built as if he used to be a fighter— broad shoulders, chiseled arms, and a flattened nose—got behind him and massaged his shoulders. "He got nothin'," he said, his voice heavy with a Spanish accent. "This *cabron* ain't got a god damn thing for you, Champ!" The trainer spoke in broken English instead of his native language. He was either sending a message to the TV cameras, or to Michael.

Michael turned toward Dutch. "That bastard's loud, isn't' he?"

A smile briefly broke over Dutch's face and he forced back a laugh. "I haven't heard a thing."

The referee called both men to the center of the ring. Cortez was excitable, bouncing around like someone high on meth, screaming, "you're dead" and "I'm gonna kill you, punk" as the ref went over the rules. Michael breathed deeply through his nose, mouth sealed tight, and his heart pounded as he tried to focus on Cortez. He found his eyes darting here and there, at the corner of the ring, up at the lights, at the referee's pale forehead and receding hairline, then his bow tie and crisply pressed blue shirt. His instincts so wildly contradicted themselves-- *run, fight, wait, puke, piss yourself, kill, die*-- it felt like his muscles would tear themselves apart.

"Touch gloves and come out fighting," the ref said. The two men bumped fists and returned to their corners. Dutch grabbed his fighter and sat him down.

"Breathe," the old man said to the amped-up fighter as he smeared Vaseline on Michael's face. "Breathe." Michael let slow jets of air out of his mouth. "Good. Open." Michael opened his mouth and Dutch slipped the mouth guard in. "I want you to let him hit you."

Michael raised an eyebrow at his trainer. "Are you fucking insane?" he said, muffled by the mouth guard.

"Michael, look where you are. This is the big time." They took a second to look over the standing-room only crowd, filling up one of the biggest and most famous arenas Las Vegas had to offer. The MGM Grand, the goddamned MGM Grand. "You need to take a shot or a hit or something to calm your ass down," Dutch said. "Since I can't give you vodka or weed, you need to take a shot on the chin. You need to see that this is happening and happening right now."

Michael tried to wrap his mind around what his mentor just said. "Hit me?" he said, rolling the concept off his tongue. "Let him hit me." It was English for sure, but it still didn't sound right.

"Feel him out," Dutch said. "Let him take his one best shot, a freebie. After that, just let him come to you. Don't chase him. Don't play his game, play yours. Pray." Michael quickly faced the corner and dropped to one knee. In his head he recited the prayer Dutch taught him years ago.

Dear Lord, don't let me fuck this up.

"Seconds out," the referee called and Dutch maneuvered through the ropes, taking the stool with him. "Okay, Mike, you're on the clock," he said. "Time to make the doughnuts."

The bell rang and the two fighters approached center ring. Cortez stepped toward Michael, staying a hair's breadth outside of Michael's reach and circled him, sizing him up. Michael stood his ground and kept turning to face Cortez as the Champ continued to dance around the ring. Michael took a few deep breaths and the salsa dancing girls in his stomach finally went away. He slightly lowered his guard and beckoned Cortez with his glove.

"Come on, motherfucker," Michael said, muffled by his mouthpiece and slightly heavy breath. "Come get it." Cortez smirked and stepped toward Michael, poking at his defense with his left hand – once, then twice more – as Michael slapped the weak exploratory jabs away. Cortez backed up a couple of steps, and then stepped in with the left jab again, hitting nothing but leather.

"Press him!" Cortez's trainer yelled from his corner. "Hit him, god damn it!"

Cortez stood his ground and jabbed at Michael's defense with the left, but he stepped back and leaned out of the way. When Michael popped back up, Cortez's right cross was there, glancing off his chest.

Michael took a couple of steps back, took a breath, and set himself. Cortez advanced slowly while weaving and leaning with his upper body, still measuring him out, and twice tapped Dane's glove with the left hand – pop-pop. Cortez brought his right hand up and Michael covered his face.

An instant later, Michael felt leather pushing hard against his ribs, driving the air from his lungs and forcing him back a step. Crowd noise like television static filled his ears as Cortez planted two hooks on his ribcage. Michael wrapped his arms around Cortez and took a couple of deep – and surprisingly painful – breaths as he gauged how hurt he was. *Not seriously,* he thought, *but damn.* No one had ever been as aggressive or as confident in their tools to try to end him in the first round. No one's ever hit him that hard.

Holy shit, he thought, *this is for real.*

The referee separated the two men and ordered the fight to continue. Michael took a couple more deep breaths and smiled as he stepped towards his opponent. The salsa girls were gone.

Cortez approached Michael again and popped him twice from the outside with the right hand, both times glancing off Michael's shoulder. Michael leaned back, got his hands up and tight around his face and Cortez's quick hands touched nothing but leather. When he tried to lean forward and counter, Cortez's glove would stop millimeters shy of his face.

"Come on, Mike!" Dutch shouted from the corner over the increasing din of the crowd. "You're going to have to eat one to get out of there!"

Michael took a deep breath and lowered his hands below his neck. He rocked back as Cortez leaned in, and as the champion's darting left jab narrowly missed his nose, Michael planted a left on Cortez's chest. He leaned forward again, leading with the left, and as Cortez tagged him with a right hand to the chin, Michael planted a left hand on Cortez's right eye. Cortez staggered back a step and Michael stepped back and out from against the ropes, resetting his offense and getting his legs back underneath him. He took four clean shots from the Champ, and he was still standing. Dutch was right.

The ten-second bell sounded and Cortez circled Michael to the elated cheers of the crowd, and Michael already knew he'd lost the first round.

Chapter Five

Michael slumped onto the stool in his corner and spit his mouthpiece into Dutch's hand. He took a deep breath-- in slowly through his nose, out slowly through his mouth-- and looked Dutch in the eye. A sharp pain shot through his ribs as he inhaled and turned his field of vision momentarily red.

"You with me, kid?"

Michael nodded. The sting in his chin was fading and a quick survey with his tongue told him he still had all his teeth. The crowd's buzzing filled his head in the spaces between his breaths. The pain in his ribs mercifully began to subside.

"That was it," Dutch said as he smeared a fresh layer of petroleum jelly on Michael's forehead and chin. "You took four of his best shots. He had his chance to put you down, and he didn't take it. We're going to spend the next half-hour making damn sure he regrets it."

Michael nodded again and looked over Dutch's shoulder at the Cortez camp across the ring. Cortez had a full crew -- a head trainer, a cut man and a corner man -- and all three of them were shouting something at him, two of them in Spanish. Michael watched as Cortez breathed heavier, snarling like some kind of caged animal. Dutch never liked that environment. *The only voices in the room should be mine and mine*, he always said.

The old man grabbed Michael's face and re-centered it on him. "You got to focus," he said over the growing crowd noise as he applied the cold End-Swell iron to Michael's chin and jaw. "Cortez is good, real good. He's better than anyone you've fought. Period. But he's predictable. He's got a go-to move. And it's always going to be setup with the left to the body, then finish with the right hook up top. Every fight, it's setup with the left, finish with the right hook. It's quick, too, like lightning. You survive the right hook, he's got nothing." Michael nodded and closed his eyes. He saw the moment as crystal clear as he had seen it in every Cortez fight he watched. Left-right, bong-*bong*. And it dropped every opponent he ever faced. Survive the right hook. *Yeah, right.*

Michael opened his eyes and Dutch was still talking, though the voice was muted, garbled and blended with the crowd noise. The pretty, dark-haired ring girl holding the Round 2 card above her head was doing her strut around the ring, her smallish breasts mashed together in a glittery, tight silver bikini. He watched her individual muscles flex as they moved her across the ring, from feet and ankles to calves, thighs and hips. It was a well-conducted symphony that made many of the men in attendance whistle and cheer distinctly over the rest of the crowd.

Dutch grabbed Michael's face and again centered it on him, his fingers sliding in the slick jelly layer on Michael's skin. "You listening to me, champ?"

"Protect the body. Disrupt his rhythm. Don't let him set you up."

Dutch was silent for a moment as the ref called "Seconds out!" from the center of the ring. "I hate when you do that," he said as he slipped the mouthpiece into Michael's mouth and slid out of the ring. "Act like you've done this before," he said.

☆ ☆ ☆

In direct contrast to -- almost in defiance of -- the lucrative side interests of its CEO, Inferno Enterprises Inc. was a legitimate business that took up the 12th, 14th, and 15th floors on the northeast side of an office building at the corner of Broadway and West 16th Street, just north of the West Village. The floors were divided by department: Music and Media were on the first level, Talent and Management on the second level, and the Executive Office -- Dante's office -- was on the top.

Michael sat in Dante's office alone with the lights off. While Boone and Dante talked in the conference room next door, Michael gazed out the enormous picture window and watched the sun set behind Broadway. The streets' lighting changed gradually and subtly from bright yellow, natural light, to red, blue and green neon. Traffic stuttered along Broadway as the late evening rush began.

Michael tugged at his shirt to try and cool off, even though the building's climate control kept the office at a constant and comfortable 68 degrees. He tapped his foot impatiently on the elegant red maple hardwood floor and tried to imagine exactly what the hell they could be talking about that was so private, especially after the day Boone had just put him through. The image of that Jamaican guy, a bullet-riddled, bloody mess on that rooftop was burned into his brain. Every time he thought about it, he had to suppress the urge to throw up again.

Then he thought about standing over Quin Cortez's prone body with the light-heavyweight championship in hand, and the urge went away. He even forced a smile. *Title shot,* he thought, fidgeting in his seat. *That's what all this is about.*

He had come a long way in the last few years, when Dutch had him fight in converted gyms and night clubs as they tried to build a profile. Dante approached him after a club fight, where he annihilated one guy in a minute-six. He was offered a contract, more money than he had ever seen, with a $10, 000 signing bonus up front. He took it on the condition that Dutch be his trainer. He should have been wary when Dante started asking for favors. Drive to this place. Drive this car. Drop this off. Little things, here and there.

Then came the night he got pulled over driving one of Dante's cars. He had no idea about the gun in the glove box.

Dante's lawyers got a seven year sentence cut in half, him being a first-time offender and all. He only served two years. He never once rolled on Dante.

Title shot.

The soft whoosh of the oversized glass doors opening woke Michael from his daydream. Dante strode in and sat behind his desk, swiveling his leather office chair toward the floor-to-ceiling windows. Michael looked around the room and realized they were alone.

"Where's Boone?" His voice trembled slightly and he shifted his weight in the seat. The rhythm he tapped with his left foot slowed with fatigue, so he kept the same rhythm with the other foot almost without interruption.

"I told him to go home," Dante said. "It's been a long day."

"You're telling *me*."

Dante turned toward Michael and drummed his fingers on the desk in time with Michael's toe-tapping. When Dante slowed his pace down, Michael did as well and they both stopped simultaneously after a few seconds. "Yeah, about that." He took a deep breath. "Boone told me everything before I let him leave."

I bet, Michael thought. The temperature in the room seemed to drop five degrees. Michael could've sworn he saw frost coming from Dante's mouth.

Dante reached inside the drawer of his polished, lacquered cherry wood desk and pulled out a bottle of tequila and two shot glasses. He filled both glasses and offered one to Michael, who shook his head no. "Take it," he said. "You need to relax. Salut." Michael looked at Dante for a moment, then at the glass. With a deep sigh, he took the glass and downed the shot.

"Good." Dante picked up his shot and knocked it back. "I'm always surprised at how much tequila tastes like shit," he said. "It will get you fucked up pretty fast, but the road there is never pretty."

"Not really in a space to taste tequila right now Dante," Michael said. "I'm freaked out about what happened today. I'm not going back to prison, man. No way."

"Easy, easy," Dante said. "I got you, man. Nobody's going to prison. Don't worry about it. Everything will be--"

"When do I get my title shot, Dante?" Michael looked at the inside of his shot glass for a moment before his gaze met Dante's. "I've done everything you asked of me. I've been patient. I've beaten everyone you put in front of me. Set up the fight." He tapped his glass on Dante's desk. "Hit me again."

Dante poured two more shots and set one in front of Michael. Dante downed his shot and shoved his cigar back in his mouth. "Barking orders at me is a bad idea." Cigar smoke billowed from the corners of his mouth. "I'm not your employee. You don't get to tell me what to do. Maybe we let the fact that I think you're cool cloud the nature of this relationship. I got you out of prison. I fund your career. You work for *me*. You owe *me.*"

"I'll keep that in mind if I'm ever asked about two dead Jamaicans on a roof in Washington Heights." Michael didn't blink as he spoke to Dante. "I work for *you*. Got it."

Dante took one final pull on the cigar before putting it out with a twist in the ashtray on his desk. "So," he said, without looking up, "it's like that?"

"It's like that. I'm a fighter, not a thug." Michael stood up took the shot of tequila sitting in front of him and knocked it back.

"I'm not doing this anymore for you Dante. That was it. I don't want to go back to prison. But if I have to -- and this I swear to God -- I'll put you all there with me if you don't stop fucking with me and get me my title shot."

Dante looked up at Michael and smiled. "Well played. You learn well. You took a bad situation and turned it to benefit you."

"Whatever," Michael said. "I couldn't care less about situations and lessons. Or your cheap shit tequila. I want my title shot."

Dante nodded and poured himself a third tequila shot. "Okay. I'll make it happen. Start training." Dante threw the shot back and hacked a few times. "Now get the fuck out."

The bell rang for the second round and the two fighters stalked their way to center ring. Cortez charged in again led with his left jab—two taps Michael's defense—and launched the power right hook at his opponent's head. Michael got his hands up just in time to deflect the right, and the sharp slap of leather on leather echoed in his ears. The bloodthirsty crowd erupted as the Champion went to work on the Challenger. Cortez continued his attack on Michael's defense; his powerful punches at first came in fast and sounded like gunfire as hook-and-hook then cross-and-hook combinations pounded against Michael's gloves and forearms. After a few seconds at that relentless pace, the punches slowed down. Cortez tried to throw his hook around Michael's shell defense, but missed as Michael weaved out of the way. *He's still looking to end this early,* Michael thought. The respite was momentary, and Cortez again rained staccato jabs onto Michael's forearms. Michael backed up and jabbed his way out, sticking one on the Champion's body and one on his face, then following with a stiff right that caught the attention of the crowd.

"Come on, Champ!" Cortez's head trainer shouted. "Play small ball! Set him up! Mix up your punches!"

Cortez took a quick step back and a deep breath before he closed the distance and tapped twice at Michael's defense with the left jab. He stepped back again and worked behind the jab at a more controlled pace. He seemed to pick his spots and measured distance with his jab. Michael tried to return fire between Cortez's shots but none of his jabs found a home, and Cortez immediately doubled up on the left jab to the body. Michael scrambled back a couple of steps and set his hands in front of his midsection to protect the body.

"Keep those damn hands up!" Dutch shouted from the corner as Cortez peppered Michael's defense with jabs. He inched closer and Michael tapped his body with a jab, keeping himself at the end of Cortez's reach. When Michael dropped his left hand to jab, sweeping right hook found its way through Michael's guard and only narrowly missed his face. Michael leaned forward and landed a jab and a right hook, backing Cortez up a step. Michael crept forward and measured Cortez with his jab, testing his opponent's seldom-used defense. Cortez's hands protected his head, and the odd jab slipped in to the body.

"Double time, Mike! Double up" Dutch shouted from the corner. Michael flicked the left faster, popping twice on Cortez's gloves, and homed in on his body as Cortez tried to weave away. The champ deflected the shots to the body and Michael switched targets, sticking three clean jabs to the face. Cortez slipped past Michael's next jab and as he came up for air, he was met by Michael's well-timed right hook.

Cortez spun around and landed on one knee. He quickly regained his feet and charged at Michael with a scream only to be held back by the referee. Michael was ordered to a neutral corner as the ref completed a perfunctory standing eight-count on Cortez. A knockdown -- only the fourth in the champion's career. The crowd exploded to its feet. A smile cracked Michael's face despite his best efforts to keep his business face on.

The 10-second warning sounded as the referee ordered the fight to continue. Cortez charged from the corner as if he were shot from a cannon; Michael barely had a moment to get his hands up as Cortez threw hook after hook at Michael's defense. A couple of them found their way through the tight guard Michael had around his face. The bell rang and the referee had to pull Cortez away. Michael heard him scream over the roar of the crowd, "You got lucky, punk! I'll kill you! You're dead! Dead!"

Ten Weeks Earlier...

Michael spotted Boone's shiny black GMC Yukon Denali outside his apartment building from a block away and cursed aloud. *Just when I thought I was done with this asshole.* It had been a couple of weeks since they had seen or spoken to each other, the last contact being a voicemail from Boone saying that Dante set up a Vegas fight against Quin Cortez for Halloween. Michael didn't return the call.

The dark-tinted passenger window rolled down as Michael approached the vehicle and there was Dante, smoldering cigar in hand. He wore his customary three-piece, this time a black suit with a purple shirt and red tie, undone and slung loosely around his neck. It was apparently the end of a long day. "Get in the truck," he said calmly, looking straight ahead out the windshield. Michael hesitated and Dante turned toward him, a stern look on his face that made the instruction fall somewhere between polite request and direct order. "Now. Please."

Michael closed his eyes and sighed aloud. "Fuck," he said as he slid into the back seat. He hated being in that truck. Every time he saw that charcoal-colored leather interior, something bad was about to happen, like roughing up a junkie, or murdering drug-dealers in cold blood. Michael felt his stomach skip rope and the familiar feeling of an approaching dry-heave crept ever closer. He fought it back; as much as he hated the car, he'd probably hate cleaning it at gunpoint more.

Boone pulled out of the parking space and cruised at drive-by speed down the block. "I'm training," Michael said. "We couldn't do this over the phone? I don't have the time to be--"

"Stop talking," Dante said. "Listen to me. Cortez's people are looking to sell his contract. Something about him being too difficult to book at a profit. Irony is, though, that his contract is only valuable to me while he's champion. He's such a dick that no one wants to fight him without a title on the line."

Michael stared blankly at Dante and tried his best not to say "And? What does this have to do with me?" Instead, he blinked twice and said, "Wow. Good for you. Well, I have to get back to training."

"I'm not done," Dante said as he puffed the cigar a few times, took a deep drag, and then blew a mouthful of smoke out the passenger-side window. Michael tapped his foot impatiently. "Like I was saying, the contract is only valuable while he's champion, and quite frankly nine bookies out of ten pick you to win the fight. Three-to-one." He laughed for a moment. "That's hilarious. Three-to-one. They even think that Cortez had been *ducking* you."

"I don't follow," Michael said. "Why is that so funny?"

"I'm betting against you," Dante said. "A hundred grand. The contract is up for sale for three." He turned around in his seat and looked directly at Michael. "I'm going to need you to lose this fight."

Chapter Six

Michael leaned back in his seat and stared Dante in the face, raising an eyebrow and cocking his head. He turned his attention briefly to the neighborhood as they rolled by. Storefronts closed because of the late hour. Apartment buildings had gone dark as the tenants slept. Michael opened his mouth as if to say something, but the breath caught in the back of his mouth. He cleared his throat and started again. "I don't think I heard you right," he said.

Dante turned back around in his seat to face the windshield. "I'm sure you did," he said calmly. He puffed on his cigar and then took another deep drag.

Michael turned his head to the front of the car. "If I did, it sounded a lot like you were saying you wanted me to throw this fight."

Dante glanced over at Boone then at the windshield again. "Not wanted, *needed*," he said, exhaling thick gray smoke. "And yeah, that's pretty much it."

After a moment, a smile broke over Michael's face. Then that smile turned into a laugh. Dante and Boone joined. "This fuckin' guy," Michael sighed, then laughed after a moment. "Seriously, what do you want?"

Dante's laugh gradually subsided. "Oh, crap," he said. "You still don't get it. Maybe I wasn't being clear. I need you. To lose. Your next fight."

Michael leaned forward in his seat. "Have you lost your mind?" he said through tightly clenched teeth. "What in the world makes you think I'm going to lose? This is the fight I've been waiting for my whole life. I've been training, working my ass off for years for this fight. I'm in the best shape of my life. How do you expect me to do that?"

"Sixth round. Fall down. I don't see what's so complicated."

"Fuck you," Michael snapped. "Stop the car." He turned and reached for the door handle as the SUV cruised to a stop alongside the curb. "I don't fall down for *nobody*. I'm too good of a fighter for that. If I lose, I lose. But it happens straight up."

Dante laughed. "Are you serious? You haven't fought a straight up fight in three years."

The last three years of fights blurred through Michael's head as Dante finished his sentence. Every punch he threw, every hit he evaded, every time he stood over a fallen opponent in triumph came rushing back. A lump rose in his throat. "You're lying," he said.

The smile left Dante's face. "Wait," he said shaking his head, "you didn't know? Don't tell me you actually thought you were *that* good. I mean couldn't you see it? Couldn't the old man? Everyone you fought to this point was either a has-been, or a never-was. Some former big names, good enough to put on a show, but no actual contenders. And they *still* took dives."

"No. They stepped in that ring. They fought me. I beat them. You can't fake that."

"Sure you can. I told them to take dives. I offered them money. I told some of them to make you look good, and I told some of them to make you sweat a little. In the end, they fell when I told them to." He took one last pull from the cigar, held the smoke in his mouth and exhaled out the window. "Face facts, superstar. You, your career, your life, that's all my creation. You do as I say. You get your shot when I say it's time."

Michael stared at the floor of the car. His arms were crossed, and he clenched his fists until his knuckles turned white. His teeth were gnashed so tightly they threatened to break under the pressure. He glanced over at Boone's stoic face, took a deep breath and stared Dante in the eye. "Now that I know this, what's stopping me from telling someone?"

Dante laughed, blowing the lingering odor of just-smoked cigar in Michael's face. "Who are you going to tell? The boxing officials? They'll revoke all your fight licenses. You'll never fight again. The police? I happen to know things too, Mike. I know that you're an accessory to that gruesome murder in Washington Heights. I know that you played major parts in several illegal, drug-related activities." He flicked the cigar end out the window and pressed the up button. The window whirred shut. "Come on, killer, don't look so surprised. And stop being so self-righteous. If I had told you your fights were rigged while you were winning, I'm sure you wouldn't have had so big of a problem with it. Everyone has to lose sometime, kid."

Dutch guided his fighter into the corner as Michael watched Cortez rant and rave from across the ring. The crowd was still buzzing at the early knockdown from late in the second round, but Michael could barely hear it over the sound of his own heaving breath. His heart was beating at a mile a minute, so hard he could feel it throbbing in his temples.

"Snap out of it, Mike," Dutch said as he sat his fighter down. "We only have a minute!"

"Protect the eye, wait for an opening," Michael said.

"We're not there yet." Dutch slapped the End-Swell on Michael's left eye, ironing out a mouse that had begun to form.

"He's still getting some of them through," he said. "Tighten up your defense up top. You don't need to have any kind of swelling near your eyes. He's fast enough without you going blind. Mouthpiece."

Michael laughed a little and spit his mouth guard into Dutch's hand. Dutch rinsed it clean with his squirt bottle and shot some water into Michael's mouth. As he swished the water around in his mouth, Michael looked across the ring at his visibly angry opponent. Cortez focused on Michael, refusing the between round clean-up work his corner was trying to do. He snorted like an angry bull and Michael could see every muscle twitch and tighten.

Michael spat out his mouthful of water. "He's pissed."

Dutch glanced over his shoulder at Cortez. "Yeah, he is," he said. "You showed the world his ass. He's going to let his anger control him for a moment. Don't fall for it; he's trying to intimidate you." Dutch slipped the mouth guard back into Michael's mouth. "He's still dangerous, though. Don't take this lightly. He's got a mad-on and you just painted a big red target on your forehead. This guy is a loaded weapon."

"Which is it -- don't fall for it, or don't take it lightly?"

"Seconds out," the ref called. Cortez's corner cleared out and the champion stood up, bouncing on the balls of his feet and glaring at Michael.

"Get out there," Dutch said, rolling out of the ring and taking the stool with him. "Protect the eye. Wait for an opening."

The crowd exploded as the two fighters approached the center of the ring. Michael bounced and rolled his neck back while Cortez stalked back and forth on his side of the ring, glaring at his opponent snorting frequently. Cortez charged straight for Michael once the bell rang, nearly running over the referee to get there. Michael got his hands up and felt three of the champ's shots sting his forearms and biceps as he tried to weave out of the way. He wasn't sure how many Cortez threw, but the champ was swinging for the fences. Michael felt the rush of air that followed a hard right cross blow the sweat off his brow.

He peered over his defense as he took a hop-step back. Cortez didn't chase; instead, he inched forward one step at a time, flicking out the jab when Michael stopped moving. Michael tried to slide-step left and Cortez cut him off. Michael stood his ground and threw his weight behind a left hook. He then advanced when Cortez leaned out of the way. Michael worked behind his left jab and tried to extend his arms and keep out of Cortez's reach. The Champ got his hands up to block, ducked and weaved around two of Michael's lefts and closed the distance between them by a step or two.

"Double up, Mike!" Dutch shouted from the corner over the rising clamor of the crowd. "He's getting too close, double up!"

Michael snapped out two short jabs and both of them landed harmlessly on Cortez's forearms. He doubled up again, this time forcing the second one between the gloves to Cortez's nose. Cortez went stiff for a moment as Michael landed two more jabs on his forehead. The packed arena seemed poised to detonate when Michael shifted his weight and lined up the right hook.

The world seemed to slow down when Michael saw Cortez lean back and away from the right. He put so much weight behind the punch that the whiff forced him forward a step. Cortez smiled as he lowered his left hand and landed an uppercut to his chest and folded him in two. An overhand right to the jaw made his legs go wobbly. Gravity soon took over and Michael found himself face-down, drooling on the canvas.

Michael's eyes fluttered open. He stared at the ring's bottom rope and waited for the ringing in his ears to stop. His arms felt like they were encased in lead and his legs like they were made of cardboard. He saw people in the crowd jumping in the air, open-mouthed, probably screaming. It all sounded like white noise to him. Flash bulbs exploded in the crowd like little flares, adding to Michael's dizziness. He turned his head toward Dutch, who was slamming his hands on the mat and screaming "Get up!" It sounded like Dutch was talking underwater.

"Three!"

Michael turned his head toward the referee who stood over him, counting. His voice came in loud and clear. Michael could hear the rising commotion of the capacity crowd.

"Get up!" He heard Dutch shout again. He sounded much clearer this time. Michael reached for the bottom rope with his left hand and pushed himself up with his right. When he got to his knees, he put both hands on the canvas and pressed up as hard as he could.

"Four!"

Michael got his feet underneath him and stood up. He took a wobbly step forward, nearly falling again, but caught himself and remained upright. The ref finished his eight-count and grabbed Michael's wrists. "Are you okay?" he asked as he tried to push his wrists down. Michael turned his head toward the skyboxes. It was dark up there, but he could just barely make out a glowing orange dot. Michael glared at that spot, grinding his lower teeth against his mouth guard.

"Are you okay?" the ref asked again. Michael nodded and kept his wrists tense.

The ref ordered the fight to continue, and Cortez bounced out of the neutral corner, staying just beyond Michael's range. He leaned his head in, and as Michael flicked his jab out, Cortez pulled his head back. Michael hit nothing but empty space. Cortez smiled and did it again, making Michael miss. The crowd started to boo and Cortez danced around the ring, staying just a hair's breadth outside of Michael's reach.

"He's making you look stupid out there!" Dutch shouted. "Get after this punk!"

Michael shortened the distance between them, connecting with a leading left hook and following up with a quick left jab that Cortez avoided. The hook hit hard and Cortez stopped dancing. He nodded his head, smiled and simply said "Okay," as he stepped back into the fight. Michael kept Cortez a safe distance away and popped out double shots of his jab as the champ snuck closer. Cortez put his gloves up around his head, ducked down and charged in.

"Hit him!" Dutch shouted from the corner. "Hit him now!"

Michael dropped his left hand and whipped a sharp hook around Cortez's defense to his head. Cortez popped up and countered with a short-armed uppercut to Michael's body. Michael landed the hook again on Cortez's head and followed it up with a strong left jab, while Cortez wrapped a hook around his ribcage. The crowd got louder as Michael dropped in another jab and a right cross then stepped back to avoid a murderous uppercut headed for his chin. He retreated two steps then took a step forward with his left jab to meet an advancing Cortez. Cortez absorbed the jab to the head and wrapped Michael up in a clinch.

"You got nothing, chump," Cortez said as Michael tried to wriggle free. "Why don't you just lay down like a good little patsy?" Cortez stomped Michael's left foot, out of the ref's sight and shoved Michael away from the clinch just as the 10-second warning sounded. Cortez bounced back two steps, popping Michael's defense with jabs. As the round ended, he landed a huge left hook right on Michael's navel. Michael doubled over and stumbled toward his corner.

"Chump," Cortez said as he passed by.

Another round to him.

49

"Fuck you, Dante." Michael's cheeks puffed out as he breathed. "I don't give a shit who you have a deal with. I'm not taking a dive, and you can't really make me."

Dante shook his head. "You see, that doesn't work for me, "he said. "So it doesn't work for you. But if you need some incentive, so be it. If you don't lose this fight like I tell you to, there will be tragic personal consequences."

"What the hell does *that* mean?" Michael said. "You'll kill me? That the best you can do?"

"For starters. Then maybe your old buddy Dutch. Or that preggo ex of yours. Selena." Dante took a deep breath through his nose, then exhaled. "You seen her lately? She looks like she's ready to pop."

In one swift motion, Michael reached around the front passenger seat, hooked Dante's throat with his forearm and pulled his neck against the headrest. Dante hacked and coughed as Michael leaned in toward his ear, tightening the hold. Without taking his eyes off the road, Boone drew his gun, pressed it against Michael's temple and released the safety.

"Leave her alone," Michael whispered. "You hurt her and I'll kill you."

Dante motioned toward Boone and the big man put the safety back on. "I guess that's up to you, isn't it?" he gagged.

After a moment of listening to Dante choke on his own saliva Michael released the hold. Dante coughed as he regained his breath and Boone put the gun back in its holster. The three of them sat in silence for a moment.

"So do we have a deal?" Dante asked.

Michael sat back in his seat, arms folded, breathing hard. "I need two things from you," he said, not looking up. "I need fifty grand."

"You're getting a hundred grand from your fight purse. Why am I giving you fifty?"

"To keep me from going to the cops."

Dante smiled and shook his head. "Okay. And the other thing?"

"I need your word that you'll leave Selena alone. She stays out of this. Her and the baby. This is between me and you. She stays safe, understood?"

Dante laughed. "I'm giving up my leverage? Why?"

"To keep me from killing you in your sleep. I know where you live Dante, and Boone won't be around to protect you all the time." Michael looked up, meeting Dante's eyes in the rearview mirror. "Your word."

Dante's smile vanished. "Fall down in the third to signal that you're on board." The rear passenger door clicked open. "Now get the fuck out."

Chapter Seven

Dutch slapped the End-Swell on Michael's jaw and pulled the mouth guard from between his teeth. Michael rocked his jaw back and forth but the swelling and stiffness made it uncomfortable. His ears still rang from the shot that put him to the canvas and his knees still felt wobbly. He saw that overhand right in his head again and again, each time slower than the last. That last shot he took wasn't his finest moment. Michael braced himself for the words of wisdom Dutch would impart for the next round. The old man would probably lay into him for failing to keep his hands up or for allowing himself to be put on his ass with so much on the line. He was surprised by Dutch's silence as the old man knelt beside him and ironed out the swelling in his jaw. Then again, what was there to say?

Dejected, Michael turned his attention to the center of the ring as the blonde card girl with the surgically perfected breasts strutted with the Round 4 card over her head. She seemed to force her chest out as she held the card aloft, which gave the hooting and hollering men in attendance a show and made the knot that tied her glittery bikini top work overtime. Just past her, in the Champ's corner across the ring, Quin Cortez seethed. He snorted and rocked back and forth as his corner men worked on him. His head trainer screamed at him in Spanish – not Michael's first language, so it was hard to eavesdrop. Michael picked out a couple of words here and there, like *matanza* (kill), *muerto* (dead), and *agolpamiento* (crush). But had no idea what they were actually saying until the trainer uttered something Michael had heard before.

"Él no tiene ningun corazón!"

It sounded only a little different than the last time he heard it. Loosely translated, it meant "he has no heart."

☆ ☆ ☆

Eight and a half months before...

Selena Arguello was Michael's favorite drug.

She stood a statuesque five-foot-eleven, the only woman he had been with that he could look directly in the eye. Her skin smelled of sunshine in the summer and fresh-fallen snow in the winter; her complexion went from caramel in the early fall to mocha by the end of spring. She was a mutt, a mix of the most desirable features of every flavor. The bone-straight, jet black hair she got from her one-sixth Cherokee ancestry hung down to her waist and would hover around the middle of her back when she had it in a ponytail. Her slightly narrowed, slanted, dark eyes sat above a small, pointed nose, freckled cheeks, full, pouty lips and an impossibly straight natural smile. She had perfect, hand-sized breasts perched above a flat midsection. From the ground up, her legs were powerful and toned with muscular yet feminine calves and thighs that ended at a heart-shaped ass that was both enticing and intimidating.

Being part Ecuadorean, she rolled her R's while she spoke and instantly redirected men's blood flow southward. And being part Brazilian, she came equipped with a short-fused temper with a hair-trigger.

When they would fight and break up, Michael would have night sweats and spontaneous itching. He was irritable when they weren't together, a bitch to be around and nearly useless in the training ring. He would swear he'd never go through that again and start to recover. But after a couple of weeks, sometimes maybe a month, he'd relapse. An hour with her made his heart and brain soar higher than snorting three lines of cocaine. That same hour could calm his nerves like six shots of vodka, or mellow him out more than a lungful of bong smoke. She never quite got what she did to him, and he could never understand why.

It was two weeks after their last fight when Michael saw the missed call on his cell phone. His neck itched even before he checked the text message.

NEED 2 TALK. COMIN OVA @ 8.

They'd played this game several times over their two years together. When she wanted to apologize, she would text "need to talk," and when he wanted to apologize he'd text "I miss u." Michael knew he would forgive her; he decided it when he saw the missed call. The only question was how long he was going to make her sweat.

He nearly tripped over himself to answer the door, and there she stood on the other side in a black leather jacket and stylish winter boots. She wordlessly walked in and tossed the jacket on his sofa, revealing a blue sweater that gently suggested her feminine shape and blue jeans that proclaimed it. Michael's mouth watered.

"We need to talk," she deadpanned, dispensing with any conventional greeting.

"Excuse me?" he said with fake hurt in his voice. "You don't even say hello? You just walk past me? In my own house, no less?"

"Oh god, I'm sorry," she said. She gave him a long, tight embrace that made his knees buckle. *Yeah, I'll make her sweat, maybe for a minute,* he thought. *And then, make-up time.* His thoughts went directly to the amazing make-up sex they seemed to have on a semi-regular basis and wondered if he had remembered to fix the creak in his bed. "I'm just so worried and--" She took a deep breath and broke the hug. Her eyes were glassy when she finally looked him in the face. "We need to talk."

Michael was stunned by the idea she might *actually* have something to say this time, and not the normal song and dance that came with her usual apology. She had something *important* on her mind. He watched as she sat down on the sofa and wiped a tear from her face. *Crying?* he thought. *This can't be good.* He took a deep breath and braced himself. "What is it?"

She looked up at him and burst into rolling sobs. "I'm late," she bawled. "I'm sorry, but I'm late."

Michael checked his watch: eight o'clock, right on the dot. He relaxed. "Actually," he said, "you're about three minutes early. It's only just now eight. And even so, it's nothing to cry about, baby. I forgive you."

Selena laughed through her tears. "God, you're a fucking idiot." She smiled and took a deep breath. "I'm pregnant." She looked Michael in the eye with a mask of tears and mascara streaming down her face.

Michael would have shouted "What?" if he weren't choking on his liver as it tried to crawl out of his mouth. He hacked and coughed, tears now running down *his* own face as he tried to force the organ to make a decision – in or out.

"I-I don't know how it could have happened," she said, words coming out faster now. "I mean we-we were so careful, so so careful, with the condoms and birth control and all of that - I mean, we were safe, but now I'm a couple weeks late and normally that isn't something to worry about, with stress and all but I had a feeling and took a test I bought from the pharmacy and the little thing came up blue and those are supposed to be accurate but I took another one and it showed a plus sign and I think that means I'm pregnant, and we're having a baby and--" She brushed her hair out of her face and looked up at Michael, who could only offer a blank stare in response. "You're scaring me," she said. "Say something."

Michael stared at her a few more seconds, unable to breathe. "Is it mine?" he asked, as if the words had been dislodged from his throat by someone using the Heimlich maneuver.

She cocked her head to the side for a moment before her eyes jumped wide and narrowed just as quickly. "Of course it's yours," she snapped. "What the fuck kind of question is *that?*" Her dark brown eyes smoldered through her tears. A vein on her forehead throbbed and she huffed quick breaths.

"A good one," Michael said matter-of-factly. He could hear her short fuse sizzle.

"Well, who else's could it be?"

"You tell me. I didn't see you in the couple of weeks where you 'needed a break.'" He punctuated the phrase with air-quotes. She hated air-quotes. "We both know what happens when you decide you want a break."

"Who the hell do you think you are?" she hissed. "Don't you dare make me out to be some kind of crazy slut, okay? You're the one who couldn't keep his dick in his pants, who had these *meretrizes* calling you all hours of the night with me in your bed!" He wasn't sure what the word meant, but he assumed it wasn't flattering. What he knew for sure was that he shouldn't have gotten turned on when she said it, but he did. She looked at the ground and closed her eyes, trying to catch her breath. "Look," she said looking at him again, this time with cold anger in her eyes. "You want to ask me something, be a man and come out with it."

"Are you fucking around?" Michael asked. "Is this my baby?"

The accusation knocked her back in her seat. "Wow," she said as tears again poured down her face. She wiped under both eyes and took another deep breath. "This was a bad idea," she said as she put her palms on her knees and pushed herself up. She grabbed her coat and fumbled her arms through the sleeves. "I'm gone."

"Wait a minute, you're holding *that* against me?" Michael said as she walked past him. He got up and cut her off on the way to the door.

"Get out of my way, Michael."

"You tell me you need a break, we don't speak in weeks, and now you tell me you're pregnant and I'm not supposed to ask you a question like that? You *dare* me to ask you, and you expect me not to? You get pissed when I do?" He grabbed her by the shoulders firmly and held her in front of him. "Come on, babe, that's crazy! What did you expect me to say?"

Selena paused a moment before grabbing Michael's face. She kissed him gently on the cheek and whispered, "Fuck you" into his ear. She kneed him in the balls hard with those long and toned Brazilian legs and got out of the way as he doubled over.

"We're done," she said. "Over. It's finished. I'll do this on my own. I don't want nothing from you. Nothing." She threw her weight behind a hard right hand that found its mark on Michael's jaw, and in that moment as he found himself face down on his hardwood floor, he regretted teaching her that punch. "You could never be this baby's father. You're not a man. How can you be a man? *Tú no tienes corazón!*" She said that as she slammed the door behind her.

Loosely translated: "You have no heart."

* * *

Dutch grabbed his protégé's mouth piece and shoved it into place. "I want to believe you're giving me all you got," he said as he smeared Vaseline on Michael's face. "This is round 4. He's got two more before he's in uncharted territory. But if you're not going to fight, let me know now. We won't answer the bell. I'll throw the towel in."

Michael's lips curled up in a sneer. "You do that, old man, and I'll kill you."

"You don't decide to stand up and fight, he'll kill *you*. Don't make me watch that. Figure it out. Now. My first job is to protect you, and if you don't fight, I'm stopping it."

The ref called for the trainers to leave and Michael stood up from his stool. Dutch slipped under the bottom rope and took the stool with him. The crowd noise rose in anticipation and Michael turned toward his corner and looked Dutch in the eye. "Don't stop this," he said.

Dutch grabbed the bottom rope and pulled himself closer to his fighter. "Then show me something."

Chapter Eight

Cortez's murderous left hook found a home on Michael's jaw; it nearly turned his head completely around as he stumbled back. Michael somehow regained his balance, steadied himself on wobbly legs and cautiously stepped back into the fray. He led with the left jab and narrowly missed as Cortez leaned back and rolled out of the way. He stepped toward the champion again and tried to find the range with the jab, but Cortez slipped out of the way.

"Double up!" Dutch called from the corner over the ever-growing excitement of the crowd. Michael flicked out two quick jabs; Cortez ducked the first, deflected the second with his shoulder and weaved his way the extra inch into the range of his own jab. Michael tried to hop back, flashing out another jab, but the champion beat him to the punch and stuck a pair of stinging shots to the chest. Michael quickly got his hands up near his head, took a step toward Cortez and shoved him back.

The challenger flared out jabs to keep Cortez at the end of his range, then took another step forward and flicked out three more quick shots, none landing. After the third, though, Cortez tagged him twice solidly in the ribs with his left jab and sunk a right uppercut into the side of his face.

Michael had never studied the lights in an arena before – not closely, anyway. But he was sure there weren't supposed to be quite so many of the big white flood lamps circling the ring as he saw. There were supposed to be 20 or so he thought, but it seemed more like 60 hovering above him -- wait, 40? But by the time his head finished snapping back, it was back down to 20. He leaned against the ropes and sprung forward, throwing his arms around Cortez for a momentary rest. His left eye hurt like hell, but he was still able to see, mostly. Teeth? All still there. Jaw? Ringing, but he didn't think it was broken.

"Come on, goddammit," he heard Dutch shout from the corner over the rising cheer of a bloodthirsty crowd. He glanced over his shoulder and saw his friend with a white towel at the ready. Michael heard panic in Dutch's words. "Fight back!"

Michael pushed out of the clinch just as the referee came in to break it up. He pounded his fists together, took a deep breath and got back to work. Cortez strode toward him and confidently stuck the jab on Michael's chest. Michael got his arms up and in front of him in time to knock the next shot out of the way and quickly bull-rushed his way inside Cortez's range. Cortez stepped back and again used quick jabs to keep Michael at bay as the challenger short-armed a jab to Cortez's midsection. Cortez threw three quick jabs in a row – pop, pop, pop – that hit Michael's gloves and were followed by a short-armed left hook that again landed on Michael's ribs. The crowd "ohh"ed their approval as Cortez hopped back a couple of steps, half-circled around Michael and advanced again.

Michael snaked out his jab to keep Cortez at the end of his reach. Then he stepped back and circled, waiting for Cortez to advance. When the champ closed a little distance, Michael threw a quick jab and followed it with a stiff right that landed right between the pecs and elicited an even louder "ohh" from the crowd. Michael circled again, moving his hands up and down snapping out the left jab every few seconds to keep Cortez away.

"Don't fight scared," Dutch shouted again from the corner, slamming his hand on the mat. "Take it to him! Come on, kid, take it to him!"

Cortez stepped forward and absorbed a jab to the face as he landed a left hook to Michael's midsection. Michael tried to retreat, but the champ closed in quickly, pounded away on Michael's midsection with hooks and the odd uppercut, all to the cacophonous approval of the mob.

Michael got his hands up and elbows in to protect his body, turning his waist to deflect some of the power shots that took his breath away. As fatigue started to slow down Cortez's assault, Michael short-armed a left hook into Cortez's chest, followed by a quick jab-hook combo. He planted another couple of shots on the champ's ribs before Cortez dropped his head, ducked down and stepped back. Cortez's retreat was brief as he took a quick breath and attacked again. He pounced on Michael with a jab to the body, and pounded away at Michael's ribs with the right uppercut and hook.

Michael skipped back a step and rolled away as he and Cortez circled the center of the ring. He heaved through some labored breaths and deflected Cortez's incoming left jab. He forced pained breaths through his nose as he circled Cortez. The champ doubled up on the jab and popped Michael's leather as he slapped the punches away. *Get through the round,* Michael thought. *Stay upright, get through the round.*

Michael deflected Cortez's power left hook and fired out the left jab on his chest. He swayed his upper body forward and back, and when Cortez stuck a jab on him, Michael hit him with two quick lefts and a right hook to the body. Cortez landed a hook on Michael's eye, and Michael landed two more on the champ's body before their arms tangled in each other. Cortez hooked his fists around Michael's arms and took a deep breath as the challenger tried to wriggle free. Cortez got one hand loose and punched

Michael in the gut as the 10-second warning sounded and the ref stepped in to separate them.

Michael inhaled sharply and exhaled slowly as he stepped toward Cortez. His arms felt like lead noodles as he tested the champ with more jabs. Cortez slipped past the first two, but as the third one connected to his chest, he fired back with a quick jab-hook combination just as the round ended. As they walked past each other to their respective corners, Cortez shoulder-bumped Michael and glared at him.

"Get your eyes checked, chump," he said as a malicious grin spread across his face, "and watch where you're going."

Michael shoved back and the referee got in between them, pushing them back toward their corners.

"Fuck you!" Michael yelled, waving his fists as the crowd got excited. "Try that shit again and see what happens, tough guy!"

Cortez laughed and pointed his hand to his ear as if he couldn't hear. Dutch got in between Michael and the ref, grabbed his fighter by the shoulders and shoved him down onto the stool. "Sit down, shut up, listen," he said as he slapped the cold, steel End-Swell on Michael's rapidly swelling left eye and pressed hard. "You've got to fight now, *right now,* as if your life depended upon it. Because it does." With his free hand, he slid Michael's mouth guard out, put it on the mat and doused it with water. "If you don't, he's going to beat your ass bloody."

Eight and a half months earlier...

Dutch blew his whistle to end the round. "Time," he called, and Michael and his sparring partner Eddie Strickland touched gloves. Eddie was one of Dutch's newest fighters and only had three professional fights under his belt, but he was much stronger than as his lanky yet toned frame suggested. He had tagged Michael in the chest with a right hook that he threw like a bolo whip just before Dutch ended the round.

"God damn it," Dutch shouted. "The Carlton fight is three weeks away and you're still weak on your left!" He shook his head and walked around the ring as Michael took a breather in the center. The small crowd that gathered around the Basement Ring of the Dewey Street Gym cheered and whooped and a couple of women called to Michael and snapped his picture when he turned around to acknowledge them.

"If you're going to do that shit," Dutch snarled at the photographer, "at least turn off the fucking flash!" Dutch pulled Michael close as he came back to the corner. "You keep dropping your left," he said, slapping at Michael's left glove. "Carlton is heavy on the right hook. If you keep dropping that left, *he* will drop *you*. For the last time, *please*, keep the fucking left up."

Michael smiled and his mouthpiece slid out. "Every time's the last time with you, man. You should chill out before you have a heart attack."

Dutch shook his head and massaged the bridge of his nose. "Are you gonna work today or what?"

"Oh come on, Dutch. I'm just trying to make this look good. You know, give these people a show."

"What the hell is that supposed to mean?" Dutch's brown face went purple and spit flew from his mouth.

"Yo, Mike!" a voice from the back of the Basement called. He looked up and saw a young man waving to get his attention from the brick wall at the opposite end of the room, near the steel staircase. "My girl don't believe me," he said as he held up his smartphone. Michael smiled and flexed long enough for the guy to snap the picture.

"Okay, to hell with this," Dutch threw his towel into the ring. "Training's over. Everybody get out." Dutch climbed out of the ring and walked past the crowd, herding them toward the stairs at the far end of the Basement.

Michael stared at him for a moment as he walked out, then turned back to Eddie, who shrugged and ripped the tape off his gloves with his teeth. "Whoa," Michael said as he hustled out of the ring toward his mentor. "What's this about?"

Dutch didn't break stride to look at Michael. "The one thing, the *only* thing I ever asked of you since you were a kid was to not waste my time," he said. "You don't take this seriously, you can get hurt. You can do that if I'm not here, so it makes no sense for me to be."

"Dutch, please." Michael stepped in front of him and stopped him with both hands. "All this ain't necessary. I mean, it's just sparring. We both got headgear on. Just relax a little and have some fun." Michael laughed and shadowboxed in Dutch's general direction. He bounced, bobbed, weaved, and jabbed at the space in front of his trainer.

The old man slapped Michael's fist away, hard enough that the sound echoed through the Basement. "Have some fun?" He spewed another cloud of atomized saliva in his immediate vicinity. "Are you that fucking stupid?" Dutch seethed for a moment before he took a couple of deep, calming breaths. "Every time you step into a ring, there is another guy in there who can hurt you," he said solemnly. "Every time, someone can kill you if you're not sharp with what you're doing. Even during sparring. Even with headgear. You're good, Mike." Dutch shook his head and took another deep breath. "You're damn good. But even *you're* not good enough to dick around and show off." He grabbed Michael's head and looked him square in the eye. "I don't know if you realize this, but the men you get in the ring with are not only trained to take inhuman punishment, they're taught how to kill a man using only their hands as blunt instruments. They train sixteen hours a day to do it. They're paid very well to do it. You're not taking this seriously. You're not prepared. As your trainer, I can't let you fight."

Eddie walked right past them as they talked. "Ok, I'm gone, guys," he said.

"See you later, Eddie," Dutch said, waving at him.

"Whoa," Michael said, grabbing Eddie's arm. "Don't go nowhere just yet."

"Let him go, Mike. We're done for today."

"No we're not. You can't cancel the fight. It's in three weeks. We need to keep sparring. I'll be okay, you know. You worry too much. It's all good. I got skills."

Dutch took a step back and looked over his pupil. After a moment's assessment, he shook his head. "No. I wish you did. You got talent. There's a difference. Skill beats talent every time."

Michael let Eddie's arm go and stared at Dutch in disbelief. "What the fuck is that supposed to mean?" he said. As he closed the distance between him and his mentor, he wore the insult with a raised eyebrow.

"If I have to tell you," Dutch said, walking around Michael to the stairs, "then you got bigger problems than this next fight."

"Oh come on, save the Yoda bullshit!" Michael shouted after him. "Dante said this would happen, you know."

At the mention of Dante Alexander, Dutch stopped in the stairwell and turned to look at Michael. He made no secret of his distaste for Dante, and the fact that Michael invoked the man's name in his presence stiffened his spine. "Oh, did he?" Dutch looked down at his fighter from four steps up. "The great fight guru Dante said this would happen?"

"Yeah, he did. He said you would see the truth, old man. That I'm better than you were. I'm better than my dad was. That eventually it would get under your skin and the jealousy-"

"Jealousy?" Dutch stomped back down the four stairs that separated them and got nose-to nose with Michael. "Everything I have ever done for you was to make you better. You think I did all that training for my sake? All those 12, 14 hour days, rebuilding you when you got out of prison, you think I did that for me? And where the fuck do you get off talking about your dad like that? Are you better than I was? Hell yes. But your father?" Dutch shook his head and took a deep breath. "Stephen Dane was my best friend, and the most gifted boxer I'd ever seen. He understood that his hands were his weapons of war. He was a better man, too, and he would put a punk like you under the ring for disrespecting his art like this."

Michael took a deep breath and stepped back as he looked Dutch squarely in the eye. "He was a burnout, a junkie and a drunk," Michael said. "He was abusive and absentee. He died drunk trying to rape my mom right in front of me. In the end, she clubbed him upside the head with a metal baseball bat and I watched as his skull split open. Great man he was, huh Dutch?"

As soon as he said it, Michael regretted it. Dutch sighed deeply and looked up to the ceiling. "Maria, Stephen, I'm sorry," he said solemnly. "I tried." He once again looked Michael in the eye. "I love you like a son, Michael. But fuck you. I quit." He turned and walked up the stairs. "Get out of my gym."

☆ ☆ ☆

Sharp pain shot down the side of Michael's face as Dutch ironed out the swollen eye. Michael hissed through his teeth and grunted. "Little Chihuahua ass motherfucker," he said, breathing heavy. "Can't believe he cheap-shotted me like that. Fucking punk ass-"

"Shut up." Dutch took the steel bar off Michael's eye. The shiner was flattened some, but his whole left eye was now dark and puffy. Dutch upended a bottle of water over Michael's head and slapped a bag of ice on the back of his neck. "He ain't gotta respect you! He's the champ!" Dutch's tone rose in both harshness and volume as he spoke. "Who the fuck are you? Huh? He's beaten fifteen guys like you since he's been champ, guys with talent, guys with skill, and he beats them down!" He smeared Vaseline on what was left of the lump over his fighter's eye. "You think you deserve respect? You gotta beat it out of him! You gotta hit him and hit him and hit him until he's got no choice but to take you seriously!" Dutch was fully riled up now, shaking and spitting as he spoke. His face turned a disquieting shade of purple. He sucked air through the small spaces between his teeth as he grabbed Michael's head looked at him eye-to-eye. "The only thing you got going is that you're in the fifth round. You get past this, and he's in uncharted territory. He's in your house. You've fought marathons, he hasn't. You've gone eight, nine, ten rounds before, with guys bigger and meaner than this sumbitch! Win this round and he's gotta come after you!"

"Seconds out," the ref called, and the crowd in the arena buzzed with anticipation. Small pockets of the audience chanted Cortez's name as his trainers got him to his feet.

Dutch slid the mouth guard back into Michael's mouth. "How's the eye? How's your sight?"

Michael breathed in deeply as he nodded and got to his feet. "I'm good," he said.

"Guard that eye," Dutch said as he stepped under the bottom two ropes, taking the stool with him. "It's a big fucking target."

Chapter Nine

Nine weeks earlier…

H e scrolled to her name a dozen times on his phone, and a dozen times he hung up when the call was about to connect. Michael didn't know how he was going to do this, no clue what he would say, but he needed to talk to her. Their relationship had always been volatile, true, but the last time they'd spoken was just ugly.

Tú no tienes corazón, she said to him, their parting words. He had called her a liar, she called him heartless. All because she said she was pregnant.

Yeah, he would have left too.

He stared at her name in his cell phone one more time, his thumb hovering over the green "call" button. "Call her," he said out loud. "Maybe she wants to talk too." Michael took a deep breath and hit the button. The other end rang for what seemed like an hour, the longest three rings he had ever heard, before the voice mail came up.

"Hey, this is Selena. Leave a message."

It was the best possible thing that could have happened; he wasn't sure what he would have said to her if she had picked up, but he was sure it would've been awkward.

"Hey, it's Mike. I--" He took a couple of bottomless breaths. "I'm not sure what to say here, really. You probably hate me. You're probably right to. And the last thing in the world you want to do is hear my voice. So if you haven't skipped this by now, thank you."

Jesus, he thought, *this is ugly.*

"Look, I'm calling because I want to talk. I--" He froze for a moment, thinking of the words to say that would make her understand. What would he tell her? That his promoter was a criminal? That the same promoter basically used him as an enforcer? That his entire career since he got out of prison was a lie? It was a lot for one voice mail.

He sighed deeply into the phone. "I need to talk to you, to see you. Please. Just call me back, okay?"

She'll never understand, he thought as he ended the call and choked back a tear. He wasn't sure he understood it either.

The bell rang and Michael moved tentatively toward the middle of the ring, keeping his left hand high around his slightly swollen eye. Cortez met him half way and shifted his hands from high to low, swaying his body back and forth. When he got close enough, Cortez threw a jab at Michael's body, then hopped back out. They half-circled each other again before Cortez leapt in to throw another jab. As the jab hit Michael's body, he landed one of his own on Cortez's nose. And when the champ's head snapped back, Michael followed with a right to the body. He quickly closed the distance and landed two hard hooks to Cortez's chest, and was met with a straight right to the puffy left eye. Michael scampered back outside of Cortez's reach, pounded his gloves together and stepped back into the fight. He popped at Cortez's defense from the far end of his range and his punches hit nothing but leather as the champion deflected the incoming jabs.

Cortez stepped toward him and flicked out with a left, then another, both times hitting Michael's gloves. Cortez skipped back a step as a feint then charged forward. As his right hand came up, Michael's guard went up reflexively and Cortez stepped in closer, slipped a jab underneath the defense to the body, and followed it with a straight right. Michael dropped his guard to protect the body and was greeted with a stiff left jab to his jaw and a right cross on his nose. Michael stumbled back a couple of steps and found himself on the ropes, tucking his head to his chest and trying to fend off Cortez's assault.

"Punch out, kid!" Dutch yelled from the corner as the crowd cheered in anticipation. "Don't get lazy on me, Mike, punch out of it!"

Michael got his hands up around his head and leaned forward. As Cortez connected with a hard right to his body, Michael shoved him back and stepped out of the corner. Once out, he jumped back two steps and kept Cortez on the outer end of his reach. Michael shot out one jab, two jabs, and as he shifted weight to deliver a right hook, Cortez closed the distance on him. He ducked under Michael's hook and landed a left uppercut to the body. Cortez followed with a straight right to that puffy left eye and sent Michael backwards to the mat.

Michael took a deep breath as he stared up at the arena lights again and soon, their brightness temporarily obscured by the ref's bald head. *Get up,* he thought as the ref counted. *Don't stay down. On your feet, boy.* By the count of four, he was on his knees. He was upright by the count of six and after checking to see if he was okay, the ref waved the fight to continue.

Michael bounced twice on the balls of his feet and headed straight for Cortez, who took a step back and playfully beckoned him with his glove. Michael led with the jab and aimed one at

Cortez's face that hit leather. He swayed his body back and forth again, snapping another pair of jabs at Cortez's face each time he leaned forward. The first time, Cortez knocked them back. The second time, one got through.

The third time, Cortez got his hand up near his face. Michael lowered his target and planted the jab on Cortez's chest. He followed that with a hard, high right hook to the side of the champ's head. Cortez staggered and Michael pounced, getting in close and landing four hard hooks to the body. Cortez grabbed both of Michael's arms for a clinch. Michael could hear Cortez's labored breathing, and as the referee came to separate them, Cortez pushed out of the clinch.

Michael immediately closed the distance between them. He felt Cortez out at the end of his reach, planting a couple of jabs on his chest and stepping back. Cortez absorbed the shots and chased after Michael, getting back inside his comfortable range and scoring with hard hooks to Michael's ribs. The crowd started to bubble with excitement as Cortez wailed on Michael's midsection, too close for the contender to pull his arms in and cover up.

The 10-second warning sounded as Cortez landed an uppercut to the middle of Michael's torso. The shot drove the air from Michael's lungs and dropped him to one knee. Cortez landed one more blast to the side of Michael's head, just above that swollen left eye, a moment before the referee pulled him back. "What, chump?" the champ shouted at Michael, voice muffled by his mouth guard. "You got nothing for me, son! Nothing!"

The ref came over to Michael after Cortez was in the neutral corner. Cortez was still shouting over at him, and the crowd noise sounded like radio static. Michael was still on his right knee, trying to find the footing in his left to push up and stand. "You okay, Mike?" the ref asked. The ringing in Michael's ears partially muted the ref's voice. "Can you continue?"

Michael pushed up with his back leg and his fist. He stumbled back a step, then forward and looked the referee in the face.

"Can you continue?" he asked again.

Michael wasn't sure whether it was sweat, blood or drool running down the left side of his face, but he figured there was no way he looked good if the ref was asking if he could go on. It was painful to open his eye, and everything on his left side was blurry and gray. "Please don't stop this," he said. "I'm fine. I'm fine. Don't stop this."

The bell rang as the referee looked across the ring to Michael's corner. Dutch had the stool out in an instant and was ready to receive his fighter. "Can you make it to your corner?" the ref said. "You get to the corner okay and I won't stop it."

Michael looked up and saw two of Dutch, one in color, the other grayscale. He lined himself up between them, lumbered to the corner and collapsed onto the stool. The referee walked behind him and spoke to Dutch. "He's taking a beating out there," he said. "If he doesn't defend himself, I'm stopping it."

"Come on, not in a title fight," Dutch said. "Let them fight! He gets up, right?"

"Fix that eye, Dutch," the ref said as he walked away. "It's leaking all over the place."

"You hear that, Mike?" Dutch said as the referee left. "You drop that left and this is what happens!"

"I fought him," Michael said. "I fought back."

"Not enough. You gotta win rounds. Start winning rounds. Box the man!" Dutch pressed the end-swell hard on Michael's eye, directing the fluid toward a small cut just outside the eye. Michael hissed as the cold steel pushed on the sensitive skin, but the eye numbed up quickly and he soon felt the trickle of blood down his left cheek turn into a faster flowing stream. Dutch quickly mopped the blood off his face and swabbed a Q-Tip with coagulant against the wound. He smeared ointment on the area and stepped back. "It isn't pretty. Should get you through the next round though. How's your vision?"

Michael blinked quickly. His eye still hurt like hell, but he wasn't seeing double anymore. Everything was still a little blurry, and he couldn't see in complete color, but he was able to pick out the gray cloud across the ring as Cortez.

"I'll be okay," he said.

"We're still not out of this yet. Round six now, kid. It's our time. He's never been here before, but you have. You got the guts, you got the wind, and I sure as hell know you do because I trained your ass."

"You believe in me, Dutch?"

Dutch took his fighter's mouth guard out and squirted water into it. He opened Michael's mouth and shot a mouthful of water in. "Hell no," he said with a smile as Michael rinsed his mouth and spit. "Prove me wrong."

Michael hadn't seen Dutch since the old man quit more than six months earlier.

It had been years since he'd been back to Smith Street and Dutch's two-bedroom duplex. He remembered the first time he set foot in the door. It was the summer after he turned eight, his mother was in prison for murdering his father, and Michael had nowhere else to go. Dutch always told Michael the truth about his parents, about how his dad was a scrapper who got close but never quite made it and how his mother was a sweet woman who didn't really have murder in her heart.

Michael stood outside Dutch's apartment and stared at the big brass number one on the door. *I probably should have called first,* he thought. He paced back and forth, turned to leave then stopped at the corner, turned back and stopped in front of the door.

Then again, what exactly is there to say except for what I'm here to say?

He glanced at his watch; it was 11:30 p.m. He had come after stopping off at the gym. The training took on a whole different feel for him after the meeting with Dante the day before. His trainer's methods seemed to be more lax, his style more forgiving of mistakes. The sparring session that night was a joke. The guy they had him training against was old and out of shape, and Michael found himself silently begging his partner to fight back, while his trainer lauded him with compliments. Michael stuck a jab-hook combo to the sides of his partner's headgear, and the old guy went down.

"Come on, fight back," he yelled. "Jason, get this guy to fight back!"

"It's low-impact training," Jason Troy, his trainer said from outside the ring. "He's not supposed to fight you." He reminded Michael of one of those guys in baseball, the sabremetric guys. Young guys who had the game reduced to numbers, but never actually ever played. "Cortez is weak in his combo defense. The third power hit of every combo thrown at him lands 18% more than the first two. Work on stringing together combos, get the muscle memory up to speed."

"Muscle memory is for focus pads," Michael said. "This is supposed to be live combat training. It's bullshit!"

"You'll be fine, killer," Jason said. "Okay, get up and do it again!"

The cheers of people watching him spar seemed peppered with bits of laughter, and the feeling of being at home in the gym Dante had set up for him was suddenly replaced by feeling as if he were the only one not in on the joke. His trainer was texting, his staff was holding interviews, and the sparring partner was taking punches for a paycheck. So he undid the laces on his gloves and stepped between the ropes, tossing them gloves as he headed to the locker room.

"Hey, what's going on?" Jason said. "What are you doing?"

"We're done, here," Michael said. "It's not working out. Tell Dante I said thanks, but no thanks, I'll figure something else out for training."

So Michael quit his training session, fired his head trainer and all his staff, and found himself on Dutch's doorstep nine weeks ahead of a title fight. *Talk about a Hail Mary,* he thought. He took a deep breath and knocked three times on the door. He checked his watch again. 11:32.

Please God, let him be awake.

Michael waited a few more moments before banging on the door again. He heard shuffle behind the door, and a muffled, ornery voice yell, "All right, already, calm down." The door flew open and Dutch was there, angrily snarling, "What?" The two men stared at each other for a long, awkward moment. Dutch looked Michael up and down, like a dog checking out an intruder in his territory.

"I don't want any," he said as he slammed the door and locked it behind him.

"I need to know something, Dutch," Michael yelled to the closed door. "Man to man."

"Go away," Dutch's muffled voice said. "It's late and I got nothing to say to you."

"I need you, Dutch. I need to know--" He took a deep breath. "Did you know about it?" Michael paced outside Dutch's door, running a hand over the two-day stubble on his head. "I mean, you were right. You were right about Dante, about all of it. I don't know how you knew, but damn it you did. I need to know if you knew about--" He couldn't quite get it out, and wasn't even sure his former mentor wasn't listening. He took a deep breath and turned to walk away when he heard the deadbolt click and the door creak open. He walked back over to the door and cautiously pushed it open to see Dutch leaning on his kitchen counter. "Come in if you're coming in," he said. "I don't want to let out the air conditioning."

Chapter Ten

"I suspected," Dutch said after Michael finished his story. He took a sip of coffee and leaned back in his high-backed cloth seat. His eyes drifted from the table they sat at to the window off to his left side. "I wasn't sure the fights were fixed, but you breezed through a couple of those guys way too easily. The fight against Marcus Carlton? You weren't prepared. I've seen him fight since. He should have kicked your ass all over Atlantic City."

Michael hadn't given much thought to the fight. It was over in four rounds, and in the first round and a half Marcus Carlton beat him soundly. Michael had a difficult time getting out of the way of Carlton's sweeping right hook from the opening bell. Inside of the first minute, Michael's eye was puffy. By the end of the first round he had already been put to his knees. The early parts of round two had been more of the same, and Marcus Carlton had Michael on the ropes and hammered him on the inside. Then the tide turned suddenly. He landed a shot on Carlton's ribcage that staggered him, and the man who Dutch once referred to as a shark lost his wind like a pinhole in a balloon. Michael thought that in the remaining rounds he caught his second wind and had perfectly executed the plan he and Dutch's replacement, Jason Troy had crafted. He thought he capitalized on mistakes Carlton was making. Now he wasn't so sure.

After the fight that night, Marcus Carlton came to his locker room to thank him for a good fight. He didn't look like someone who just got knocked out, but Michael hadn't given it any thought until now.

"So you weren't in on it?" Michael said, breathing a sigh of relief. "Dante wasn't paying to you keep me in the dark?"

"Hell no. I knew something was a little off, that's for sure. But I trained you to win, every time. I trained you to beat every one of those guys. I trained you like it was all for real, just in case. I've been around, boy. This is not my first rodeo. I've seen fights that were supposed to be dives end up with someone in the hospital." He took another sip of his coffee and put it on the circular brown coffee table in front of him. "So, word is Dante got Jason Troy in as your new head trainer. He's good."

"Yeah," Michael said. "I fired him right before I came over here."

Dutch laughed. "*That* was stupid."

Michael stared at the ground. "Maybe it was. But Dante found him for me, and after everything that happened I couldn't be sure if he was dirty or not." He looked up at Dutch, his eyes wide and fixated squarely on Dutch's forehead. "I can win this fight. I can beat Cortez. I know I can." Michael's voice caught in his throat and his eyes got glassy. "I need that title. Dante may not want that to happen, but I need to beat this guy. It's everything I've worked for my whole life. I'm this close to it, and I'm going to need your help to finish this."

Dutch whistled low through his teeth. "You're asking a whole lot," he said. "One, you want me to train you to win an unwinnable fight. Two, you're asking me to do it in nine weeks. And three, you're asking me to work for Dante again." He took another quick sip of his coffee. "Not going to happen."

"You won't be working *for* Dante," Michael said. "You'll be working *with* me. The way it used to be."

Dutch shook his head. "No. Sorry, kid, I love you like you're my own son, but you don't listen. I mean, look what you've become. After the way it worked out last time." Dutch took another sip of his coffee. "You did that to me after I've known you all your life. You know what it felt like to have to quit? To have you tell me I'm jealous of you? I'm tired, Mike. Truth is I'm too old for this kind of heartbreak."

Michael's head sunk for a moment. "Look, Dutch. I'm sorry for that. I really am. I got way ahead of myself, and--" He took a deep breath, shook his head, and looked back up at his mentor. "I shouldn't have said what I said. I didn't mean it and I felt horrible about it. It's happening. I can see it, and now that it is, I want this title more than I ever thought I would. It's close. And you're the one who can get me there. Not Jason Troy. Not Dante. You. After all we been through, old man, it wouldn't be right without you there. And I don't trust anyone else. I can't." Michael took another deep breath and wiped a tear from his face. "I'll do whatever you say. Anything you want."

Dutch looked at him for a moment before he slurped the last sip of his coffee. He stared at the bottom of his empty cup and took a deep sigh. "You shouldn't whine," he said after a long pause. "It doesn't suit you."

☆   ☆   ☆

"Seconds out!"

Michael got to his feet and Dutch maneuvered the stool and himself out of the ring. "Don't make me stop this," Dutch said. "I will not let you get yourself killed out there."

Michael bounced a few times on the balls of his feet and loosened himself up. "That's good," he said sternly. "I don't want to die yet." He strode out to the center of the ring and put his glove out to touch with Cortez. Cortez smirked and slapped the glove away, getting into his fight posture. Michael smiled slightly and a line of pain shot up from his jaw to his eye. The whole side of his face still felt heavy, and probably looked worse. He got his hands up near his face and shifted his weight back and forth. The bell rang and round six had begun to the crowd's cheering approval. Cortez pounced on Michael behind the jab. He glanced a hit on Michael's swollen face and missed the next jab, then the next. Cortez swung wildly with a hard left hook, missing over Michael's head and the challenger closed the distance between them. Michael planted two short-armed hooks on Cortez's rib cage, and when the champion countered to the body, Michael got his elbows out in front of him and hopped back.

Michael still wasn't seeing quite in color and Cortez still looked a bit blurry. But as Cortez got closer, Michael's vision got clearer. He was able to see the expression on the champ's face as he approached. With his newly regained peripheral vision he saw the ref circle into position to get the best view of the action. From the corner of his eye, Michael saw Dutch slam his hands against the mat and shout instructions. He stuck a jab on Cortez's chest, right between the nipples. Without missing a beat he followed up with a two quick hooks to the ribcage. He hopped back again and took a deep breath. When Cortez stepped forward once more, Michael fired a jab and then another, trying to keep him at the end of the distance.

Back up, he thought. *I don't want you close right now.*

Cortez again tried to step in tight, and Michael flicked out another jab. Cortez slipped underneath the punch and closed the distance between them, dropping his hands and attacking Michael's ribs. Michael dropped his elbows and tried his best to protect his core by swaying his body back and forth and keeping his elbows and forearms in front of those ribs. He saw Cortez suck air with every punch-– *Nothing on them,* he thought-– and Michael went on the offensive, trading blows for two or three punches, and then throwing everything he had into attacking the champ's torso. The din of the crowd swelled every time leather hit skin.

Cortez backed up as he bent his body out of the way, stealing precious inches away from Michael's reach. His back hit the corner as Michael charged. He hooked Michael's arms and held him in a clinch, then took a few quick breaths. Cortez used the hand hidden from the referee to hit Michael on the ribcage, and as the ref approached to separate them, he stomped Michael's foot and shoved him away as the 10-second warning sounded.

The ref apparently didn't see it as he waved the fight to continue, and Dutch was shouting from the corner. Michael only heard his own breathing and heartbeat as he stepped gingerly toward the champion, favoring his mashed right foot. Cortez leaned in with his jab, Michael's face just outside his range, and the challenger backpedaled a step. Michael swayed back and leaned forward with his own jab, sticking it on Cortez's chest. Michael quickly followed the jab with a right hook that found a home on the side of Cortez's head. He continued with a left uppercut to the ribs and an overhand right to Cortez's temple. Cortez fell back onto the ropes just as the round ended.

Michael walked past Cortez back to his corner and sat on the stool. Dutch removed his mouthpiece and squirted water into it. "Don't get too far ahead of yourself." A smile threatened to crack his face. "Now you've gone and pissed him off."

A sly smile spread across Michael's face. His eye and jaw still hurt and a trail of red appeared at his gum line. Dutch squirted water into his mouth and he spit into a bucket. "It's what I do," he said with an out-of-breath laugh.

Michael walked out of Dutch's apartment with a smile on his face, the first he could remember in months. Dutch hadn't agreed to train him yet, not in so many words at least, but Michael had the most encouraging sign of the night that his life would get better.

"Come by the gym in the morning," Dutch had said. "We'll see how bad your mechanics have gotten, and see if this is worth my time."

Michael had known the old man all his life. He never before had to prove himself worthy of Dutch's time and training. All that time not speaking had done absolutely nothing to blunt Dutch's anger. But they were speaking now, and with any luck Dutch would come out of his self-imposed mini-retirement and they would get back to work in the sweaty basement of that dusty old gym.

Michael reached into his pocket and looked at his cell phone. No calls. *She must really hate me,* he thought, redialing Selena's number. It rang out again, and Michael didn't leave a message. He walked to the empty Bay Ridge-bound platform at the 9th Street Subway station and waited for the R train. Selena lived in Sunset Park section of Brooklyn and the N train Express would get him there in half the time. But he wanted some time to talk himself out of what he was going to do, just in case he could come up with a better idea. Because Lord knows the last thing he wanted to do was look a pissed-off, pregnant Latina in the eye and rehash old mistakes.

By the time he rolled into the 45th Street station, Michael had no new ideas, but his resolve was as strong as ever. He hurried off the train and marched up to street level, and his fate.

When he got to her house -- a brownstone on 45th Street and 5th Avenue she shared with her mother and brother – he took a deep breath and knocked on the door. A few moments later, a short, matronly, bronze-skinned woman opened the door. Her eyes opened wide as she stood silently at the door with him. She was pretty for someone of her age, delicate features unaltered by wrinkles. She passed her sharp, dark eyes on to her daughter.

"*Buenos noches,*" Michael said politely. "*¿Es Selena en casa?*"

Her mother paused at the door for a moment before turning her head. "Selena!"

"What?" came the shouted response, muffled by distance.

"*Será venir a la puerta, alguien está aquí para ti!*"

Michael assumed she told Selena to come to the door but had no way of knowing for sure, as he used all the Spanish he knew by asking if she was home. Footsteps stomped their way from the back of the house to the front, getting heavier and louder as they reached the door. Selena's mother stepped out of the way and there she was, a different kind of beautiful. Her hair was pinned up, and Michael had forgotten how pretty she was without makeup. She was carrying low, and her pregnant belly stuck way out, forcing a slight but noticeable arch to her back. She wore a light robe over a white tank top, which exposed her baby bump. It took Michael a moment to realize the tank top was his. It took him a moment more to remember that the baby was his too.

Disgust quickly swept over her face; her upper lip curled up and to the left in a sneer. She looked him over like she would a homeless man on the subway whose stink preceded him, took a step back in a defensive posture and cocked her head to the side. "What," she said, less of a question and more of a demand. Michael didn't answer; he stood there, stunned and staring at Selena open-mouthed. He looked at her eyes for a moment, then back at her belly.

"Oh my goodness," he whispered in amazement. He tried to collect himself, but could only stare, open-mouthed at the mother of his child.

"Okay," she started to swing the door shut. "Good talk."

"You never called me back," Michael finally said, just as the door was about to close. She opened it again and he let out a sigh of relief his eyes locked on her. "I called," he said. "I left a message. You never called back."

"And you didn't get the hint?"

"You look good. I miss you."

Selena shook her head. "Nuh-uh, don't do that," she snapped. "I'm freaking six months pregnant. I'm hormonal. My back hurts, my ankles are swollen, I'm tired all the time, and I am in no mood for whatever bullshit you're trying to sell to me." She shook her head. "I can't do this with you," she said. "Not again."

"I need to talk to you. It's important."

Selena rolled her eyes and hissed through her teeth. "I got nothing left to say to you," she said. "And you said the most important stuff to me the last time we spoke."

"I'm sorry," Michael said. "There aren't enough words I can say about that. But you need to hear what I have to say. Can we talk?"

"No," Selena said. "I'm not gonna do that. But what I will do is this: I'm going inside and going to bed. I'm going to forget you stopped by. Then I'm going to raise this child without you. When she asks where Dad is, I'll tell her that she was immaculately conceived. And I'm going to close this door now. Thanks for stopping by." She closed the door softly Michael stood there, alone, until the porch light went out.

Chapter Eleven

The redheaded ring girl paraded around the middle of the ring, holding the Round 7 card high above her head. Her shimmering silver bikini made her oiled up and artificially bronzed skin eye-popping, but it was the way she stuck her chest out while walking with her arms extended that made Michael drool. That, or it was Dutch pressing out the swelling in his jaw. He opened his mouth and let the old man squirt another mouthful of water in, rinsed and spit a mouthful of red into the bucket on his left side.

"He's slowing down," Dutch said. "That's good. You're taking advantage of the openings he gives you. Keep making him pay for coming in too close. But don't get cocky out there. He can still bloody you with one punch. Keep him outside, outside, outside, *then* let him slip in and drop the hammer on him."

Michael nodded. He opened his mouth and let Dutch dump a mouthful of water into it, then bent his head forward as Dutch poured the rest of the bottle over him. A bag of ice once again found its way to the back of his neck.

"He's still gunning for that eye," Dutch said as he smeared jelly over the right side of Michael's face. "Here's what you do: you keep your goddamn hands up." Dutch slipped Michael's mouthpiece back in. "You don't want him to open that eye up. Protect it."

The ref called for the trainers to leave and the crowd cheered. Cortez leapt up from his stool and rolled his neck around to loosen up. Michael got to one knee and turned around in his corner. After a quick silent prayer he turned to face his opponent. He could feel the relentless pounding on the inside of his chest cavity and took a deep and calming breath. "Come on," he said under his breath. "Come to daddy."

Michael stood outside the Dewey Street Gym in the pre-dawn hours of that early autumn morning and stared at the peeling paint on the grey steel front door. A cool, crisp and gentle breeze blew past it, carrying the first few fallen leaves of the season. The place oozed the kind of grit and grime that almost reminded him of prison: a converted warehouse surrounded by 15 feet of barbed-wire fencing, steel window guards on all of the windows all lent to a generally oppressive feeling. The gym hadn't opened to the public yet, so the cinder block used to prop the door open in lieu of an exterior handle hadn't been put out. The only way into the two-story gym at this hour was through the Basement entrance.

Years ago, Dutch painted the Basement Door and the surrounding brick the same color so that at a casual glance, there was no door. It was his way of keeping the wannabes out. Dutch only told a few people about The Door: Michael and his sparring partners. Seeing as how he never had the same partner twice, Michael always assumed Dutch had them killed to protect the sanctity of the hallowed training ground. Michael crept down the side stairway and slipped into The Door.

The Door opened onto a landing in the stairway that connected to the ground-level part of the gym. Though the sun wasn't up yet, the street lights flooded through the front windows and illuminated the top level well enough to see. It felt cooler up there, more relaxed. The Basement, on the other hand, wasn't naturally lit; its only glimpse of natural light came in the early afternoon, when the sun hit the windows at just the right angle and focused a narrow shaft of light down the stairway to the lower level. The Basement sometimes got oppressively hot from the training and activity; the smell of sweaty athlete funk seemed to be seared into the walls. Michael walked down the uncarpeted metal staircase and past the invisible border that sharply divided the fresher air from upstairs and the stale stink of old sweat from the training area. The scent of unwashed fighter bombarded his nose and made his eyes tear.

He missed that smell.

Michael slowly walked toward the ring – a series of square blue mats about 10' by 10' and stacked three high - roped off by several velvet ropes. The ring wasn't elevated above the crowd like the pro rings in an arena; instead, the upstairs portion had a section of the floor cut out so that the people upstairs had an unobstructed view of the sparring going on in the Basement. Michael remembered being very young, watching his dad spar with Dutch when both men were in their prime as middleweights. Dutch was a much slimmer man back then, known as much for his magnificent afro and Fu-Manchu mustache as he was for his murderous uppercut and his brutal training style. Stephen Dane - Dutch's closest friend - was known for cheating on his wife, a legendary party lifestyle, and a coke habit. As a fighter, however, even though he didn't make much noise in his career, Michael's dad had a hell of a right hand. It even dropped Dutch in more than one sparring session.

Michael remembered one session in particular, after both their careers were well into decline and Dutch's hair started to go. The gym was up for sale and Stephen suggested he and Dutch buy it and train people. Dutch said it was a stupid idea, that it would never work, and that Stephen would never stay clean long enough to be a reliable business partner. They decided to settle it in the ring. If Stephen won, the two of them would buy the gym and offer training, his son Michael being the first student; if Dutch won, Stephen would buy a case of beer and two lawn chairs on the day they tore the place down. Dutch liked beer and watching stuff get demolished, so he agreed.

Stephen put Dutch to the mat in under two minutes with an overhand right. Dutch taught Michael that punch in the very first lesson.

Three weeks later, Stephen Dane was dead. His wife smashed his skull in with a metal baseball bat; he was drunk and high and trying to rape her. Michael, then just eight, was in the house. Immediately after the funeral, Dutch helped him change from his funeral suit to his gym sweats and put him to work against the heavy bag.

"You're late."

Michael snapped out of his trance at the sound of Dutch's scratchy voice, echoing from behind him at the base of the stairs. "I told you to be here by five."

"It *is* five," Michael said.

"*By* five. Meaning *before* five. Not five oh-one, which it is now. If you can't understand that, how do you expect to beat a 10-count?"

"I'm sorry, Dutch. Jeez, man."

Dutch walked up to Michael, looked him up and down, and without warning drove an uppercut into his gut. Michael doubled over and fell to one knee and coughed while Dutch shook his head. "Your middle is soft. Squishy. No strength to your core." Michael hacked and heaved as Dutch circled him. "Your breathing is gone. And you've been on that knee for eight seconds." Michael rose to his feet, still doubled over at the waist with his hands on his knees. Dutch hissed through his teeth. "What did they do to you? Eighteen years of training, gone in seven months. That's pitiful."

"Will you help me?" Michael wheezed. "I got no one else."

Dutch turned his back on Michael. "Your defenses are shot. Your core strength is wasted away. Your stamina is non-existent. I have seven months of bad habits to eradicate in nine weeks. And somehow, some way, you have less than three months to be ready for a title fight." Dutch tilted his head toward the sky and let out a laugh. "Dante was protecting you, believe it or not. He didn't have to ask you to throw the fight. Cortez is gonna murder you."

Michael closed his eyes and took a deep breath. He'd known in his heart: Dante's camp was training him soft. Jason Troy removed much of the difficult stuff from Michael's training routine in the name of saving energy for the fight. Running and bike work were replaced by photo ops and publicity, and sparring was almost non-existent. "I'll do whatever you want," Michael said. "I need to win this fight. More than anything. I'll do whatever you want. No questions asked."

"You're damn right, you will." Dutch turned back toward Michael and looked him in the eye. "It won't be easy. Or fun. Training's going to be a bitch. You'd better trust me. You will listen to me. You will not waste my time. You get tired when I say. You bitch, whine or quit on me at any time and I swear I'll kick you out and we'll never speak again."

Michael smiled and nodded. Dutch reached back to punch him in the gut again and Michael tightened his abs. The punch landed with a thud.

"Good," Dutch said. "Get your gear. We begin in half an hour."

✯ ✯ ✯

Michael let Cortez advance after the bell and stayed just outside his range, leaning back as Cortez's jab fell just short of his chin. The champion sucked wind as he short-armed his next three jabs while landing one that had no power behind it. Cortez jabbed again at Michael's body and missed as Michael backpedaled around the center of the ring. Cortez circled Michael for two or three steps then stood his ground and flicked that jab out. Michael didn't stop moving and evaded the jab easily.

The crowd's cheering grew more anxious as the fighters danced around each other. Michael periodically by held his ground and dropped his hands—even stuck his chin out—then backpedaled when Cortez set to throw his jab. Michael taunted like this three times, and every time, Cortez's jabs would be angrier, wilder. He smiled as Cortez turned red with frustration.

"C'mon, *puta*," the Champ said. "You gonna fight or what?"

Michael let one more jab miss his face and again stood his ground. He saw Cortez load up one more jab and leaned back to avoid it; when he did Cortez rushed in closer and fired off another left-right to the body. Michael rocked back and out of the way then quickly sprung forward and planted a left flush on Cortez's chest that had most of his weight behind it. The champ hopped back, slammed his gloves together and rushed forward again; he missed with the jab but followed with the right hook to the body.

The hook glanced of Michael's ribcage as he rocked back and out of the way. Michael shifted his weight and shuffled his feet as if he was backing off, but when Cortez leaned forward to chase, Michael immediately changed direction and stood the champion up with a stiff jab. The punch snapped Cortez's head back and Michael closed the distance; he dropped low and tagged Cortez's ribcage with two lefts and a right. The champion tried to lock arms with Michael in a clinch, but could only manage to grab his head as Michael drove a right uppercut into his solar plexus.

Cortez leaned forward and tied up Michael's hands in a clinch. Michael smiled as the champ sucked air. The ref separated them and ordered the fight to continue. Cortez tested Michael's defense with the jab and doubled up on it occasionally. Michael hung back and let the punches hit his gloves. Cortez stepped in closer and stuck the jab between Michael's gloves, but when he went to follow with a right hook, Michael beat him to the punch with his own jab, landing it right on his nose. Cortez stepped back and covered his face. Michael closed the distance and went to work on Cortez's body, landing a two left hooks in rapid succession. Cortez dropped his elbows and turned his body to defend himself, and when he deflected the fourth body shot, his elbow clipped Michael right on his swollen left eye. Michael felt the slow, warm trickle of blood roll down his face.

"Fuck!" he yelled as he covered the eye, prompting the ref to stop the round and check on the fighter. He removed Michael's hand and looked over the cut. The ring doctor stood up at the side of the ring in case he would have to check it, but the ref waved him off. The cut was small and not dangerous, and Michael was more annoyed than hurt. He issued a warning to Cortez's corner and waved the fight to continue.

Michael felt the tingling around his eye again as the area filled with fluid and the skin stretched to accommodate. His eye was swelling shut. He shifted his head around his gloves to get a better look at one of the three blurry Cortez's coming at him. He put his left hand up in front of his eye, blinked a couple of times and the triple champions merged into one body. He could see a single opponent, but his peripheral vision was gone again. Cortez's right hand disappeared into the darkness off to his left.

Michael saw the hand vanish as if it were in slow-motion—there one moment, not there the next—and it crashed into the

Franklyn C. Thomas

side of his head hard enough to knock him off his balance. A left hand landed flush on his forehead and as the 10-second warning sounded, Michael threw himself on Cortez in desperation.

"This is where you fall down," Cortez said into his ear while trying to use his obscured hand to land a kidney shot.

Michael smiled. "I don't fall down for nobody." He deflected the low blow and stepped on Cortez's right foot quick and hard. Cortez grunted in pain as the referee separated them, but smiled when the fight was ordered to continue. The bell rang immediately after. Cortez nodded and left his glove out and Michael touched it with his own as they headed to their respective corners.

Chapter Twelve

Eight Weeks Earlier…

It took just under a week for Michael to remember that Dutch was crazy.

That morning, after a jog clear across Brooklyn from Red Hook to a public pool in East New York, Dutch watched as Michael swam thirty laps then started him on underwater combo drills. "The key here is stamina," he said during one of the few moments when Michael was allowed a chance to breathe. "Cortez is surgical out there. He wears you down until you're tired of chasing him or defending against him, then he puts you down. It's a six round process. What we're going to do is outlast him."

Underwater speed drills: throw 120 punches in neck deep water in less than 100 seconds. Michael hated this part, especially after all the running. His limbs felt like jelly and he desperately tried to get muscle memory to rally past the fatigue.

"You got power in you, boy," Dutch said as he circled the pool. "If you can retain this power after twenty minutes of chasing the champ around, you might have an edge."

Power punching drills. Take a deep breath, dive, and throw as many hooks and uppers as you can at full strength before surfacing for air. Ten sets. Dutch made him stay down for at least fifteen seconds per set.

"I'm going to train the quit out of you. I'm going to rebuild you to the fighter you should've been. The fighter you would've been if it weren't for Dante."

Death dives. Touch the bottom of the deepest part of the pool, then surface, repeat. Ten times or drown. The deep end of this pool got to twenty feet.

"You can't quit. You can't stay down. You get up or you die. That's how it's got to be. You fight like you're fighting for your next breath."

Michael clawed his way out of the pool, coughing up chlorinated water as he surfaced. He dragged himself away from the pool's edge and desperately sucked in a lungful of fresh air. Dutch stood over him and handed him a towel. "On your feet," he said. "We still need to get back."

By the time Michael got back to his apartment, every muscle felt tight and prickled with soreness. He turned on the light in the studio and found head shots of Quin Cortez taped to his headboard, refrigerator, toilet, dining table and stove. Dutch must have had someone from the gym do it while they were training. It was his less-than-subtle way of telling Michael that for the next eight weeks, he was supposed to eat, sleep and shit Quin Cortez.

Michael smiled right before he fell atop the picture on his bed and passed out.

Three weeks into Michael's training, Dutch acted surprised he was still showing up. Every morning for those first few weeks, he would sarcastically say, "Oh, you're here?" and immediately begin with some sadistic training stunt, like jumping rope on a balance ball or punching a two hundred pound bag of wet sand bare-fisted. He would work Michael for thirteen hours a day, and at the end of the training say something like, "If you're going to quit, call me tonight. I'm tired of waking up so goddamned early."

When Dutch arrived at the gym on the 21st day, Michael was already there, soaked in sweat as he skipped rope. Michael cross-skipped and double-undered the rope and threw it down to end the session. "You're late," he said to Dutch.

A smile crept over the old man's face. "Shut it," he said. "We have work to do."

☆　☆　☆

"You still need to keep that left up," Dutch said, smoothing out the growing lump on Michael's eye. It was starting to go purple, but the eye was open more than before. "Can you still see out of that eye?"

Michael's eyes fluttered open again, and Dutch was a blurry dark spot washed out by light from above. "Yeah, I'm good," he grunted as Dutch pressed down with the cold steel bar.

"You're finally showing signs of life out there," Dutch said. "I was starting to think I wasted all my time with you." They shared a momentary laugh, and Dutch removed the bar. Michael's eye hurt, but at least he was seeing shapes and colors now. "He's slowing down. He's not finishing on his punches the way he was before. He's not following through on them."

"They still hurt like a bitch."

"Then stop getting hit by them. I swear, he's almost telegraphing them." Dutch looked over his shoulder at Cortez's corner as the Dominican's men worked on him. "I think he's starting to respect your range out there," Dutch said. "You tagged him pretty good last round. Look for him to do quick counters. He's going to hang back until you get impatient, then he's going to pick you apart."

"No he's not," Michael said. "He's coming after me."

"That would be stupid on his part. If you get that lucky, wait for him to get inside your reach and drop the hammer on him. I don't know how quick he's going to be, but it's fair to say it's still faster than you, so make your power shots count. You may not get a chance to land too many of them."

Michael nodded as the ref called for the next round to begin. He knelt in the corner and said a quick prayer, then rose to his feet and turned toward his opponent. Cortez was in the other corner, loosening up by bouncing on the balls of his feet. The arena trembled with the crowd's excitement.

"Hey," Dutch called, barely audible over the rising crowd noise. Michael turned around to him and bent down so he could hear. "Round eight of a title fight," Dutch said. "Who'da thunk it?"

"I did," Michael winked with his good eye and turning to face Cortez again.

Michael and Cortez touched gloves at the center of the ring, and when the bell sounded they charged at each other. Michael led with his jab, and stuck it twice on Cortez's chest. Cortez returned fire with a hook and missed and Michael tagged his jaw twice with the right hand, snapping his head back with each pop. He got his hands up to defend, then landed another jab on Cortez's forehead. Cortez slipped past the follow-up jab and closed the distance between them smashing a right hook on Michael's ribcage and an uppercut to the gut. Michael brought his elbows in close and twisted to fend off three more power shots to the body. Cortez took a hop-step back and moved his hands up slightly. When he stepped forward to throw the jab, Michael beat him to the punch and smacked a left on the bridge of his nose. Cortez got his hands up, tucked his head, and charged at Michael, locking his arms and holding on tight.

"Come on, champ," Michael said. "What'chu got for me? What'chu got, son?"

"Fuck you," the champ said. His breathing was heavy and mostly through his mouth. "I got plenty."

The ref came over and pulled them apart, shouting "Break it up," over the noise of the bellowing crowd.

"Bring it, then," Michael said as the ref got in between them. The ref looked at both combatants, saw they were ready, and waved the fight to continue. Cortez stepped slowly toward Michael and swayed his upper body back and forth. Michael wasn't quite able to pin him down; He missed twice with the jab and came up empty on a big left hook. Cortez ducked under the punch and darted inside his range. He targeted Michael's ribs again, landing four quick shots on them before the challenger could get his defense down to protect. Cortez hopped back and out of range when Michael finally got his arms up to defend. He circled the contender and periodically popped off jabs at Michael's defense.

After Cortez's third jab, Michael followed with two of his own, making the champion quickly step back and out of his reach. Michael pursued and leaned into a jab that found its home on Cortez's cheek. He followed that with an overhand right that turned Cortez's head around and made the champion fall forward. Michael stepped out of the way and allowed the canvas to catch his opponent.

The referee hustled Michael to the neutral corner and started his count on Cortez. As the referee counted and Cortez started to shuffle upright, Michael felt a pair of eyes, burning a hole in him from the heavens. He glanced over his shoulder at a dimly glowing orange dot. Over the smell of sweat and people and booze, he thought sniffed out the faint, distinct scent of cigar smoke. *Dante must be shitting a brick right now,* he thought as he blew a kiss to the skybox.

It made Michael smile.

Cortez made it to one knee before the referee started his count and was upright before the count of five, much to the raucous crowd's delight. Michael kept himself loose in the neutral corner, and when the referee ordered the fight to continue, the two men charged at each other like bulls.

Cortez got in close to Michael, much faster than anticipated, and pounded away at his midsection, landing three or four shots before Michael could mount a defense. Michael hopped back and got his hands up, protecting his core. He weaved around the next two straight rights. He picked at Cortez from the outside, keeping him at bay with the jab. When the champ tried to sidestep, a heavy left hook sent him reeling.

Cortez backed off a couple of steps, then gathered himself and pushed forward. He got past the jab from the outside, got into his range, and folded Michael in two with a right uppercut. Gravity did the rest.

Michael knew he wasn't hurt the moment his knee touched the canvas. *Fuck,* he thought as he got to his feet and the ref did a standing eight-count. *Can't believe I didn't see the uppercut. Lucky damn shot.* The ref checked his eyes and hands for focus and resistance and when he was satisfied Michael was okay, he ordered the fight to continue, just as the 10-second warning sounded. Cortez hovered just outside Michael's range, a red and blue mouthpiece accentuating a shit-eating grin. He dropped his hands and leaned toward his corner, anticipating the bell.

It may have been Cortez's arrogance, or Michael's realization that he could possibly lose this round, but Michael charged at Cortez and landed a straight right, a left hook, and an overhand right— pop, pop, *wham!*— in rapid succession, turning Cortez's head around as the bell sounded and ended round eight. As the champion was escorted toward his corner by his trainer, Michael noticed a trickle of red coming from the left corner of his mouth.

✫ ✫ ✫

Dante watched from the back of the skybox as Michael raised his arm to the crowd, and they gave their enthusiastic approval. He took a long, slow drag from his cigar as Michael sat in his corner.

"Shit," he exhaled, and a long gray plume of pungent smoke escaped his lips. He looked over his shoulder where Miguel Castillo on his cell phone chattering in Spanish and laughing. "Shit," Dante said again as he chomped down hard on the end of the cigar.

After another long pull, he extinguished it on the bottom of his seat and looked over at the bear-like, dark-skinned man seated to his left. "Boone, get the car," he said, exhaling gray smoke in a long low hiss. "And clean out the trunk. We may be going for a ride later."

Five weeks earlier...

Michael slipped the key in the gym's front door, surprised that he still had the strength in his hands to operate a lock after that last workout. He heard the heavy deadbolt catch and smiled; the sound had come to signify the end of a good day.

"Now this place brings back memories," a raspy voice from behind him said, stiffening his back and making him drop the keys. Dante stood less than twenty feet away with a lit cigar in his hand and wearing a black-suit/red-tie ensemble. "You, me, the old man, this place. We roughed it back then. Those were the days, huh?" He stalked towards Michael and took a slow, deep drag on his cigar. He blew thick gray rings of deeply fragrant smoke into the chilly September air. "I see we're going back to basics."

Michael's heart pounded and his arms tensed. "Dante," he said. "Been a while."

"I've been busy, you know. Less time to hang out. I haven't heard from you in quite some time either. I thought you forgot about me." Dante put the cigar back in his mouth and puffed on it. "You fired the expensive staff I put together for you. That made me a little curious. Makes a man want to check on his investment."

"I didn't trust them."

"Have I ever steered you wrong?" A smile spread across Dante's face like a glistening white oil slick. "They were the best of the best."

"Maybe," Michael said, kneeling down to pick up his keys, never taking his eyes off Dante. "But I need to be trained for this for real."

Dante laughed. "I have a $2 million contract in the works for the undisputed champion of the world," he said. "That's a lot of resources tied up in the idea that I can trust you to keep your word. I would hate to think that you would renege on our arrangement." He puffed on his cigar twice and exhaled. "For Selena's sake."

At the mention of her name, Michael ran up to Dante and grabbed his lapels. "Leave her out of this," he growled. "If she gets hurt, I swear to God--"

"You swear to God what?" Dante said, his normally cool voice getting loud and authoritative. He blew a mouthful of cigar smoke into Michael's face. "Go ahead. Tell me. You 'swear to God,' what?"

Michael took two deep breaths and loosened his grip on the jacket, then let him go after a couple more breaths. "I need to train like this is for real," Michael said. "Cortez could kill me if I don't know what I'm doing. I didn't trust your guys to do that for me."

"Now that's a reasonable explanation," Dante said. "You could have told me that." He tapped the ashes off his cigar and puffed on it again. "It seems that Cortez's manager is impressed with you," Dante said. "Wormy prick named Miguel Castillo. Can't stand the guy, but he's got a good eye for talent, if that counts for something." Dante turned to leave, and dropped his cigar as he headed toward his car.

"Leave her out of this," Michael called after him. "She's got no beef with this!"

Dante waved as he got into his car. "Trust me," he shouted as he shut the door.

Chapter Thirteen

"So now we know the bastard is human," Dutch said as he sat Michael down in the corner. "I saw the blood. If it can bleed, it can be beat." He took a quick look at the purple welt on Michael's chest. "How's your breathing, kid?" Michael took a couple of deep breaths as Dutch listened as best as he could without a stethoscope. The breaths were labored, but over the crowd noise Dutch couldn't hear any wheezing. He felt around Michael's ribs. The fighter winced once when Dutch got just under his chest, but the spot wasn't swollen much. "Ok, nothing's broken," he said. "You're probably just a little winded. If you want to stop that, then stop letting him hit you in the chest!"

Dutch slipped Michael's mouth guard out and rinsed it out with a quick squirt of water. "There may actually be a champ in you tonight," he said. "You got that round. The judges are finally paying attention. You're turning some heads. Open." Michael opened his mouth and Dutch squirted water in. Michael swished it around and spit it out to the side. He opened up for another squirt and swallowed. Dutch smeared Vaseline on Michael's face and applied a thicker layer to the still-swollen left eye. "I trained you for this," Dutch said. "I made you work not just your strengths, but your weaknesses. You had trouble keeping your left up, so you sparred with a patch over the left eye. You had trouble doubling up on your hooks, I made you stronger so you wouldn't have to. You know what you're doing, kid. I know because I taught it to you. You are a fucking weapon."

Dutch pointed to the opposite corner, where the champ's trainers were working on him. They cleaned up the trickle of blood from the corner of his mouth and rubbed out some of the swelling on his eye. Cortez's head trainer shouted instructions at him in Spanish as the crowd noise— some chanting "Cortez! Cortez!" and others screaming, "Let's go Dane!" drowned it out— and the champ responded with vigorous nods of the head.

"You're a weapon," Dutch repeated. "I'm aiming you at *him*. He can't just coast anymore. He has to fight you. So you take the fight to that cocky son of a bitch." Dutch quickly rinsed Michael's mouth guard with a squirt of water. "Don't fall down."

Michael smiled as the mouth guard was slipped back into his mouth. He turned around in his corner, did a quick prayer, and strode out to center ring. He touched gloves with the champ, and weaved back and forth to stay loose as the bell rung to start the ninth round.

Five weeks earlier...

He had tried to put her out of his mind. The training and the focus on Quin Cortez made it a little easier to do that. But two minutes after Dante drove off, Michael found himself on a train to Sunset Park and less than twenty minutes later, he was on her porch.

He pressed her doorbell once, twice, then pounded on her door and paced on her porch. He checked his watch –- 11:30 PM -– and knocked on her door again. "Selena!" he called in as loud a whisper as he could manage without waking the rest of the house or causing anyone in the neighborhood to wonder what lunatic was screaming into the night. "Selena!" he called again. "Come down here!"

A light went on in the bedroom directly above the door. The window slid open and a matronly Latina poked her towel-covered, roller-adorned head out the window. "I'm sorry, ma'am," Michael said, "but I need to speak to your daughter." The woman cocked her head to the side quizzically. "It's important," Michael said, exasperated.

She shook her head at him and said sternly, "*Mi hija es una buena chica. Ella merece mejor que lo que ha hecho.*" Michael stared blankly at her for a moment; his Spanish was terrible when people were talking that fast, but from the words he was able to pick out, it sounded like she said her daughter deserved better than him. *She might be right*, he thought. She shook her head again and turned back into the house. "Selena!" she shouted, loud enough that Michael could still hear her from the open window. "*El padre de su hijo bastardo está a la puerta!*"

Michael paced at the porch for a minute, though it felt like much longer. He had irrationally run through 10 different ways Dante could have gotten to her before he heard someone shuffling toward the door. The door creaked open and a visibly tired, obviously miserable, seven-months-pregnant woman stood on the other side.

She rolled her eyes dramatically when she saw him. "I don't have the energy to do this tonight," she groaned, still a bit groggy. "Can you just please tell me what the hell it is you want so I can go back to bed?"

Michael grabbed her by the shoulder. His eyes were wide and he was breathing heavily. "Are-you okay?" he blurted out. He took a breath to compose himself. "You're not hurt are you?"

Selena recoiled at his touch and slipped her shoulder out of his clammy grip. Her mouth hung open and her cheeks flashed red. "What's *wrong* with you?" she shouted, now fully awake and annoyed. Her shrill voice echoed in the neighborhood, and two or three porch lights came on. "Am I okay? Of course I'm not okay! I'm pregnant, I'm hormonal, it's almost midnight and you're here grabbing me and..." She took a deep breath and grimaced, cradling her baby bump. Hissing out a couple of self-calming breaths, she leaned on the door frame. Michael started toward her, hands extended as if to grab her, but Selena put her hand up to stop him. "I'm okay," she panted. "Jesus, this kid has most definitely got your sleep schedule."

Michael snorted and chuckled and so did Selena. The laughter subsided after a few moments, and Michael put a hand on Selena's shoulder. "I'm so sorry," he said. "I should have been here."

Selena shook her head. "We're way, *way,* past sorry now," she said.

"I need you to know something. Dante... he wants me to do something for him. Something big. I don't want to get into the details, but if I don't, he might--" Michael took a deep breath to compose himself. "*Fuck.* Are you okay?"

"Dante?" Selena shook her head. "You still dealing with that creep?"

"It's complicated."

"I'm sure." Selena took a deep breath and massaged the bridge of her nose. "I appreciate it, you know. You coming here, trying to warn me of -- whatever it is you're warning me about. But this seems like this is about you."

"What? No, it's not like that--"

"Yes it is. You've got your problems. I get that. But I got mine, and you need to get that. Dante isn't *our* problem, or my problem. He's yours. You say you want to be here. That problem – your problem – is not something I want here." Michael hung his head and Selena gently put her hand on his face. "Get your house in order," she said.

"I'm sorry," he said.

"No apologies. Apologies are nothing. Do something." She kissed him on the forehead and turned to leave.

"I got a fight," he said. Selena stopped at the door. "I don't know if you've been following. It's a title shot."

"I heard," she said. "Congratulations." She closed the door behind her softly and a moment later, Michael found himself once again standing in the dark on her front porch.

Michael moved his head and body from side to side as he approached Cortez, leading with staccato left jabs from long range. Cortez bobbed and weaved out of the way of the first two and deflected one more. He ducked and came up inside Michael's reach and planted a couple of quick jabs on that growing purple welt in the center of Michael's chest. The shots stung but he wasn't hit hard. The Champ was sucking wind; Cortez had nothing left on his punches.

Michael dropped back a step and flicked out a quick left jab to Cortez's chest, stopped for half a beat, then dropped two more and threw his body into a right hook when Cortez slipped past the third jab. The shot landed flush on the side of the champ's head, but only succeeded in staggering him a step back. *Dammit*, Michael thought, *dead arms*. He realized he probably had about as much left on his punches as Cortez did.

Michael stepped back and circled to Cortez's left, keeping him within his good eye's field of view. Cortez faked an approach with his shoulder and Michael dropped back another step and continued to circle. Cortez faked again and when he led with the shoulder once more, Michael popped him twice with the jab. It didn't have enough mustard to drop the champ, but it was quick, sounded good and made the crowd cheer. Michael leaned back for a beat then sprung forward, working behind the jab and landing three in rapid succession. Cortez ducked when Michael tried to follow with a right hook and rushed past the dogged challenger's guard. Cortez landed two or three shots on Michael's forearm before he finally penetrated the defense and tagged Michael's midsection twice. Cortez backed Michael into the corner and pounded away at his defense until Michael threw his arms around Cortez and hooked his elbows.

"You tired, son?" Cortez taunted as a smile spread across his battered face. He was slick with sweat, and he visibly gasped for breath. "You can't be tired. Nah, man, you can't be tired."

"Shut up," Michael heaved. He shoved his way out of the clinch as the referee came to separate them and slipped out of the corner as the fight resumed. Cortez continued to press him and slipped a left hook past Michael's defense. Michael winced as Cortez dinged the sore spot on his left side. Michael stumbled as he saw double then took a couple of steps back and braced himself on the ropes while Cortez continued to work the body.

"Get out of there!" Dutch shouted to his fighter. Michael pulled his arms in tight and shoved Cortez away has hard as he could. He side-stepped away from the ropes once he had the slightest amount of breathing room and reset his stance. He tapped at Cortez's defense from a distance with the jab and Cortez weaved around them as he closed the distance on Michael and forced him back toward the ropes.

"Now!" Dutch shouted. Michael shortened the jab into a left hook that wormed its way around Cortez's gloves to his right ribcage and then followed that with an overhand right to his jaw that landed with a sickening crunch and turned his head sharply left. Cortez's knees wobbled visibly before they buckled, and the champion dropped to one knee once again.

The ref shoved Michael to the neutral corner and began his count on Cortez, but he wasn't surprised at all when the ref stopped the count and ruled it a slip due to a wet spot on the canvas; anything else would have just been too easy. It wasn't long before Cortez was upright. The purple welt on his jaw looked darker and a trickle of blood dripped from his lip. When the official waved for the fight to continue, Cortez charged like an angry rhino and unloaded a wicked right that found Michael's puffy left eye. The challenger absorbed the shot and the pain that came with it as he countered with the jab, another jab to the body, and then a quick jab-hook combination. As the champion staggered forward, he reached out to lock arms with Michael. Michael stepped back and blocked the attempt by raising his arms up and sweeping Cortez toward the ropes with a stiff left hook. Once again the ref stepped in between the two fighters. Cortez, now with his back turned to Michael and slumped on the top rope, seemed unable to defend himself. Michael heard the ref talking to the champ.

"Hey, champ, can you hear me? You okay to go on?"

"Don't you even think about stopping this," Cortez said. "I can fight. Don't stop it." Cortez got up off the ropes and took a deep breath. He got his hands up, the referee checked them, and the fight was waved to continue.

The 10-second warning sounded and Cortez circled his way out of the corner, just outside Michael's range. His split lip poured dark red blood down his chin, and his shoulders sagged in visible exhaustion. He hung back and leaned toward his corner until the bell rang.

☆ ☆ ☆

He sat in the cold blue plastic chair, nervously shifting his weight as he tried to find a more comfortable position. No matter which way he turned, though, his ass hurt. Babies dominated the landscape. The waiting room was packed with expectant mothers in various stages of their pregnancies and new mothers who cradled their screaming infants. The scent of soiled diapers hung in the air. Parenting magazines lay scattered across the small glass coffee table.

A nurse came emerged from the back room: a short, pretty blonde who, even in unflattering scrubs, had a body that would have gotten Michael in trouble not that long ago. The name tag pinned to the pocket on her left breast said "Anna." "It's okay, Mr. Dane," she said. "You can come to the back."

"Thank you, Anna," he said. "Is she okay? I mean, I called her house, and her mother said something about baby and doctor—"

"She's fine. It's just a standard checkup. Ultrasound, some blood work, it's fine."

"Ultrasound? Where you can, you know, see the baby?" Michael swallowed hard and felt his knees go to jelly.

Anna stopped and put a hand on his shoulder. "I know it must be a little weird to be here. It's none of my business what you guys' relationship was. The important thing is that you're here now."

Michael nodded, and Anna pointed him toward the exam room. He walked through the door just as the doctor was running the ultrasound. "Everything looks normal," he said. "You must be the father."

"Yeah," Selena said, a stunned look on her face. "I'm not sure what he's doing here, though."

"I called this morning," Michael said. "I wanted to work something out, you know, get my house in order. Your mother told me you would be here." Michael walked over and grabbed her hand. "I don't want my kid to hate me," he said. "Or you to hate me for that matter."

Selena nodded and pointed at the screen. There, in clinical grayscale, was something that looked like a baby sucking its thumb. At the sound of the amplified heartbeat, Michael's eyes moistened. He fell immediately in love with the fuzzy image on the 3x5 screen.

A girl. A beautiful baby girl. His baby girl.

Chapter Fourteen

Four weeks earlier...

"It's a girl," Michael said as Dutch taped his hands. He avoided eye contact with the old man for a moment as the statement hung in the air. A wide, toothy grin painted the boxer's face.

"What's a girl?" Dutch put the last of the gauze tape on Michael's knuckles. The process that had taken the better part of a half hour and the fighter's hands now resembled giant cotton swabs, which Dutch stuffed one at a time into the Michael's sparring gloves. "What are you talking about? And why are you smiling?"

"Selena's pregnant," Michael beamed. His voice had a musical lilt to it. "About eight months. She's due after the fight. I saw an ultrasound yesterday. It's a girl."

Dutch cocked an eyebrow and stared at Michael. "I thought you and her were done."

"Yeah, well this happened just before that last fight. She first told me about it the night we broke up." Michael smiled and laughed. "I'm gonna be a daddy."

Dutch made a show of counting the fingers on his left hand —one, two, three, four, one, two, three. "Okay," he said, "I guess you could be the father. Convenient timing for this to come up though, don't you think? You sure it's yours?" Michael shot Dutch a look that told him a line was crossed. "Sorry. I'm just looking out for you. It's not like you and she had the healthiest relationship."

"Yeah, well, it's mine, okay?" Michael snorted.

"Just saying. The way the two of you have been, it wouldn't surprise me if this wasn't your kid, or if she came looking for a payday when she heard you were getting this fight."

"Drop it, Dutch," Michael's happy smile quickly gave way to annoyance. "She didn't come looking for me. Truth is she didn't want much to do with me. Can't say I blame her for that." Michael paused to take a couple of deep, tear-preventing breaths. "I went to find her. She told me at the beginning when she first found out. I was still working for Dante here and there, doing some—"Michael hesitated when it came to the description. "--stuff." He paused again for a second and saw in Dutch's eyes that he understood. "She drops this on me, and I react." Michael smiled and laughed. "It wasn't pretty. Then you and I had our blowup, and that wasn't pretty. So when it started coming back together, I went to find her."

"I bet that wasn't pretty either."

"The jury's still out on that one." The two men chuckled at that. Michael leaned back against the locker bank and stared at the ceiling. "It's so weird, Dutch. But the one last sign I needed to show me I'm doing the right thing here was sucking her thumb on that ultrasound screen."

Dutch slapped Michael in the back of his head hard enough that it echoed in the Basement. "Are you stupid?" he snarled. "You're putting a kid in the mix with this going on? Do you realize what we're doing here?"

"Training for a fight," Michael said. "We've done it before."

"No, we're training you for a fight you're not supposed to win. We're training you for a fight with a superior athlete where the end result, no matter what, will probably not be good." Dutch shook his head and massaged the bridge of his nose. "You know how I feel about fighting and love. Women weaken the resolve. How can you fight like you're fighting to the death if you're thinking about her? And on top of that, you're thinking about playing daddy? What's in your head?" Dutch looked away from his fighter and choked back a tear. "You're making this kid a target, you know that? Selena too. This is stupid, really stupid."

"I know," Michael said and the frustration hung from his voice. "It's just… well, you knew my dad better than anyone, and all I know of him is that he was a punch-drunk bastard who smoked a lot, drank too much, and beat his wife half to death. You tell me about the fighter he was, about the friend he was to you, but all I know of the man is that he smoked and drank his career away."

"The man had a few flaws," Dutch conceded with a nod.

"I know I'm no saint," Michael continued. "I know I've done wrong. I know I've made decisions in my life that have numbered my days. But when I go, I want to leave behind something, I don't know, a legacy. Something real. Better stories than the ones you told about my dad. I have a chance to do that, right now. My hands ache when it gets cold, my wrists are always sore. I may not get another chance like this." He took a deep breath and shrugged his shoulders. "Better to die a champ than to live a cheat, right? Say what you will about my dad, as flawed a man as he was, he would never have been in this spot. He was never a cheat."

A long silence passed between the two men. "And I want my little girl to be proud of me."

Dutch sat next to his fighter and grabbed his shoulder. "You want your kid to be proud of you? Then you better get to work on keeping that left up. Your defense is sorry." The two men shared another laugh and walked out of the locker room to the training area.

"You got him on the run," Dutch said as he pressed down the swelling on Michael's jaw. "You okay, kid?" His chest had gone from light caramel to blueberry colored as various small bruises inflicted over the course of the night coalesced into a giant, fist sized welt. It hurt to breathe and Michael couldn't tell if it was because he was just sore or because the ribs he couldn't guard had finally broken. He was gradually going color-blind and his left wrist was killing him.

"I'm good," he said, out of breath as Dutch put gauze over the cut on his left eye, and then quickly smeared over it with Vaseline. "I'm good," Michael repeated as he tried to breathe through the pain in his sides.

"You're lying to me," Dutch felt around Michael's rib cage. Michael tried his best not to wince when Dutch came to the lower rib on his left side. Dutch nodded when he got to it. "It's probably a little cracked, but not completely broken. If it were broken, you wouldn't have been able to get up or breathe. I'm not going to worry about it until you start coughing up blood." They looked across the ring at Quin Cortez. The champion had never been taken this deep into a fight, never had to fight this hard, and until this fight, he had never been busted open. He had crimson pouring from a split in his lip and his corner worked furiously to clean him up. His head trainer had one of the corner men pinch the wound shut while he applied a dot of super glue. Cortez never winced or flinched at the pain; he only stared lasers into the eyes of his challenger. Dutch looked back up at Michael, who met Cortez's contemptuous gaze with one of his own. A smile curled the old man's lips.

"Tenth round, right here," Dutch said. "You're almost there, and you're starting to make a believer out of me. And if you're convincing me, I think you might be convincing those judges. Call me crazy, but I'm starting to think you can do this. But we're not out of the woods yet. This is your fight. You got to step it up and take it to him!"

Michael nodded without breaking eye contact with Cortez. He could imagine the Dominican's corner saying the same thing in Spanish, that this fight is his if he steps up to get it.

"You know that cocky schmuck wasn't expecting you to be this serious a contender. He doesn't have the gas in the tank that you do." Dutch squirted water into his fighter's mouth, and Michael spit it out. It was slightly tinged red, but the next mouthful was spit out clean. "He's not going to knock you out. He doesn't have the punching power to do it at this point. Don't be afraid to take a hit or two. But for the love of God, protect those ribs!"

Michael heard Dutch's words mixed with crowd noise and the rapid-fire Spanish ranting of Cortez's head trainer.

"I know you're hurt," Dutch said. "Tough. Suck it up. These last three rounds, that's all that anyone will talk about. Long after you're dust, these last three rounds will be how you will be defined in this life. This is what they'll talk about at your funeral, this is the story they will tell your daughter."

The referee called for everyone to leave the ring and as the Spanish-speaking contingent left, Cortez flashed Michael a slight, wry smirk from the bruised left corner of his mouth that threatened to pop the impromptu superglue bandage on his lower lip. The champion nodded at Michael as he got to his feet.

Michael smirked back across the ring and hopped to his feet. Dutch pulled the stool out from under him and shouted to his fighter "This is your legacy!"

Damn right, Michael thought.

Game on.

Michael leaned in as he landed an overhand right flush on the headgear of his sparring partner, drawing "ohh's" from the gym patrons looking down at the sparring ring. The partner -- Dutch liked to call them training dummies -- stumbled back and leaned against the ropes as Michael advanced and attacked the midsection. He landed a flurry to the midsection -- jab, jab hook, step back, jab, jab, hook, upper -- before his opponent shoved Michael away. After that Michael pounced on him again. The training dummy shoved Michael back once more and fought back; he tapped at Michael's defense with the left, then slipped a right hook in the mix just under Michael's left eye.

Michael took a step back and held his eye. "Ouch! What was that about?"

"Time!" Dutch shouted as he stepped through the ropes and got between the two fighters. "Kid, how many times do I have to tell you to keep that left hand up? You're less than a month away from a title fight and you let this test dummy clock you in the eye!"

"He got lucky, Dutch," Michael said.

"Shut up!" Dutch shot back. Michael immediately straightened his posture and stopped holding his eye. "He got you. Period. Cortez does that and guess what? You lose. Period." Dutch shook his head and massaged his temples. "Screw this. I'm too old for this nonsense. The two of you, shower up."

The training dummy bumped fists with Michael and headed to the shower. As he ambled away, Michael walked up to Dutch and said, "We still have an hour tonight. We have work to do."

"We have problems," Dutch said. "You still have this huge hole in your game, and Cortez is going to exploit it. On top of that, we don't know if he's in on this whole thing, meaning he might not be carrying you. You could get seriously hurt."

"Oh, I'm pretty sure he doesn't know," Michael said. "Dante's pulling a double-cross on his handlers. They think they're selling him a soon-to-be ex-champion." Michael's mouth hung open as he said it and he mouthed the words again to himself again. *Soon-to-be ex-champion.* "Son of a bitch," Michael said as he pulled at the laces of his right glove with his teeth. "Unbelievable!" Michael chucked his glove across the gym floor and ran to the locker room.

He could hear Dutch's footfalls behind him. "You want to tell me what's going on?" When Michael got to the locker room, he snatched his cell phone out of his locker and scrolled through his speed dial. He hit the green button and listened to it ring. "Come on, come on, come on," he said under his breath.

Dutch ran into the locker room, out of breath. "What the hell is going on? Why are you running? Who are you calling?"

Michael put a finger up to silence Dutch as the ringing stopped and a man's voice came through on the other end. "Hello?"

"Yeah, what's up? It's Michael Dane."

Michael paused for a moment as he listened to the other end. "I'm sorry, who?"

"Don't feed me that bullshit, you know exactly who I am. We need to talk."

Chapter Fifteen

Michael felt his heart slam against the inside of his chest as he sucked in a couple of mouthfuls of air. The rib fracture on his left side immediately chastised him for breathing too deeply, but Michael figured adrenaline would take care of that shortly. He had been in long fights before -- some nine-rounders and even one that went eleven -- but never anything like quite this. The environment, the stakes, the crowd, everything about this night seemed bigger than the actual event. This was a classic, a war they would talk about forever with reverence and in hushed voices.

Please, God, don't let me pass out.

He strode to the center of the ring as calmly as he could, and stared the champion in the face. Cortez let a smirk creep up the left side of his face. It strained the hastily glued together lower lip and left a smudge of red on the white center portion of his flag-colored mouthpiece. He extended his fist to Michael, and the challenger laughed to himself as they touched gloves.

Respect, he thought. *What a concept.*

☆ ☆ ☆

The week before...

It wasn't the first time in the past several weeks that Selena spent the night, but Michael never fully appreciated the space an eight-month-pregnant woman took up on a queen-sized mattress until the night she literally kicked him off it. He landed ass-first on the hardwood floor and awoke to find himself staring at the ceiling.

"Ow," he said sarcastically after a pause.

Selena groaned and shifted on the bed. "Sorry," she said. "You okay?"

"I'm good. The floor's good for my back anyway."

"Ha ha. Very funny, drama queen. Come back to bed."

Michael got to his feet and pulled back the sheets. He hesitated before climbing back into bed. "You sure it's safe?"

"I make no promises. Now come to bed." Selena slid back over to her side of the queen-sized mattress as Michael got in. He re-fluffed her pillow and stuck it behind her head. She moaned again and quickly squeezed his hand, mumbling "thanks" as she drifted back to sleep. Michael lay back and stared at the ceiling until his eyelids got heavy. Right as he faded off to half-sleep, Selena's foot kicked hard against his shin.

"Ow, fuck!"

"Sorry," she replied, grabbing his hand. "Your daughter doesn't seem to want to sleep."

"Why is it she's my daughter when she does stuff you don't like?"

Selena closed her eyes and smiled. "I'm practicing for life after I pop." Michael smirked and yanked the pillow from underneath her head. Selena's head bounced off the mattress with a thud and she propped herself up slowly with her arm. "Asshole," she said, holding back a smile. "What did you do that for?"

"I'm practicing for life after you pop."

She punched him hard in the thigh and his leg went numb. "Keep it up. See if there's any life at all for you after I pop."

He laughed as he massaged his tingling thigh. "Bitch."

"You love it," she said as she curled up to him. He ran his hand through her hair as she gripped him tightly around the waist. "Is this what it's going to be like from now on?" she asked. "I mean, is this us, one big happy family?"

"This is happy?" Michael said, and Selena balled her fist again and aimed it at his leg. "I don't know," he said with a smile. "I guess."

Selena sighed and released her hold on Michael's waist. "When I was a kid, I used to believe a family was a mom, a dad, three kids, a dog, a happy marriage. But my dad left, I was an only child, and we never had a dog. Just me and my mom, and all of a sudden the whole idea of family was different."

Michael smiled. "My dad was a fighter, you know."

"You don't talk about him much."

"He's dead." The smile shrunk from Michael's face. "He and my mom used to have some epic fights. He drank a lot, used drugs some. He smacked her around pretty good when he was drunk or high. She fought back, but you know, he was a fighter. She didn't win very much. And she was okay with it, you know, she tried to love him, tried to hide it from me. Then one day he got drunk and in-between raping my mother, he took a swing at me." Michael took a deep breath and looked away from Selena. He shook his head to keep back tears. "My mom caved his skull in with a baseball bat. She's been in prison since I was eight."

"Oh god, I didn't know. All this time, and you never talked about your parents."

"Dutch looked after me since then. He made sure I went to school, tried his best to keep me out of trouble. He tried to talk me out of fighting, but I was so angry. I got into a lot of trouble when I was a kid. I mean, my parents were..." He took another deep breath and wiped a tear away. "When I wouldn't listen about fighting, well, he was the best damned teacher I ever had."

"Why are you telling me this? I'm not naming our daughter Dutch."

Michael laughed. "It's just... I respect the hell out of the old man for what he did for me, even after I did my stint in prison, you know? He took me right back in, and we got right back to work. He never judged me. He was always looking out for me. I want to be that kind of father, and I'm not sure I'm going to--" Michael stopped himself short; he wanted to say "have the chance" but there was no sense scaring Selena like that. She still had no idea what he was dealing with, what he would have to give up to be clear of it. She had just let him back in, maybe started to forgive him. He saw no reason to end that now.

Selena put her hand on his face and shushed him. "You're going to be fine," she said.

"I want my kid to talk about me, say good stuff about me. I want her to say 'Michael Dane is my daddy,' and never be ashamed of it."

Selena smiled and giggled. "Does this mean you going to teacher conferences, PTA meetings?"

Michael snorted and laughed out loud. "Why the hell not?"

"I love you, Michael," she said as she caressed his face. "And I honestly believe you'll be a great father. But I don't see this punch-drunk bastard at PTA bake sales or helping with homework."

☆　☆　☆

With two minutes left in the round, a right hook snaked its way around Michael's defense and found its target on his puffy right eye. The mouse that had formed four rounds before finally popped and a thin stream of blood leaked down the side of his face. Sweat seeped in and made it sting, but adrenaline blunted most of the pain. Michael took a deep, painful breath and looked up at Cortez, who seemed to move in slow motion. He saw Cortez start with his left and instinctively leaned back. The pain from his cracked rib slowed him down like he was moving through a pool of gelatin as he got his hands up in front of him.

Cortez's left hand glanced off Michael's glove, so he tucked his hands in and leaned forward. The challenger's left hand found its way through a hole in Cortez's defense to his midsection, and Michael threw his entire 171-and-change pounds behind an overhand right to Cortez's jaw. The force of the punch sent the challenger stumbling to the ropes and the champion down to a knee.

The crowd erupted and people jumped to their feet as the referee ushered Michael to the neutral corner and began his count. Cortez was slow to get up as the ref counted just over his head. The crowd's roar grew in anticipation with every passing second, but the champ rose from his knee before the count of six, just as Michael knew he would. The guys he had fought up to now were usually napping on the canvas by this point, but Cortez had been going at this with him for 10 rounds now; of course it wouldn't be that easy. Michael chastised himself for hoping the champion wouldn't be able to answer the count.

The referee waved for the fight to continue. As the crowd cheered on, Michael met Cortez at the center of the ring. Michael took as deep a breath as his damaged ribs would allow, then stepped toward the champion, leading with his left. A jab, then another, landed on Cortez's chest. Michael paused to defend the counter, leaned back and rolled to block Cortez's incoming left hook, then leaned forward into another jab. He leaned back again and weaved out of the way of two quick jabs from the champion. Michael then strung together a quick jab-hook on Cortez's chest. He leaned back one more time, and as he leaned forward, he heard one word over the crowd from Cortez's corner.

"Ahora!"

Cortez leaned back and to the left and Michael's leading jab sailed past him, and when Michael went to follow up Cortez ducked and leaned forward. Michael didn't even see the uppercut to the ribs that doubled him over, and the right hand to the nose landed with a crunch that turned his stomach as it sent him face down to the mat.

"One!"

From pitch blackness, the referee's count echoed in Michael's head. He was mouth breathing, never what you wanted to do in a fight. The smell of blood running from the cut over his eye and his certainly broken nose left a coppery taste in his mouth. It made him gag. *Don't pass out,* he thought as he gathered himself.

"Two!"

Michael opened his eyes. Sweat streamed into the open cut on his left eye, making him hiss through his mouth guard. He took a quick glance up to regain his bearings. He had been knocked down in the middle of the ring. The blood from his eye and nose dripped all over the Inferno Entertainment logo. This was not a place he wanted to be. He rested his weight on his forearms and pulled his legs toward his chest. The legs didn't have much strength left. His feet slipped twice as he tried to grip the canvas through his shoes and support his base. The third time, he finally felt his feet plant enough that he could bear weight on them.

"Three!"

Michael took a deep breath and pushed hard with his legs and forearms. He put his fist on the ground to steady his heavy limbs and then stumbled two steps forward when he tried to leverage himself upright. Blood soured his mouth and he instinctively spit. He was standing tall at four and by the count of six, the ring stopped spinning. He most definitely had a concussion. The referee ran up to him and grimaced as he finished the eight-count.

Michael laughed. "That bad, huh?" he said, just loud enough for the ref to hear.

"Can you continue?" the ref shot back, a smile cracking his face.

Michael nodded.

"You gotta defend yourself," the ref said. "Put up a fight or I'm calling it."

"This late in the fight? You're crazy. I can still go."

"If you say so, Michael, but I'll call it."

Michael leaned in closer to the ref. He could feel the thin but steady stream of blood flow from his nose to his mouth. His eye felt heavy and wept blood down the side of his face. "Don't you dare," he said, blood spraying off his lips toward the ref. "Don't you fucking dare."

The referee stepped from between the two fighters and waved the fight to continue just as the ten-second warning sounded. Michael shook the cobwebs out from his knockdown and shuffled toward Cortez. The champion approached Michael and sized him up, leading with his jab at Michael's bleeding eye. He stuck the first and the second blows on the wound, driving sweat and salt into the cut. He leaned into the right cross, but at the last moment, Michael got his hands up to deflect the blow and quickly countered with a left hook and right hook to Cortez's ribs.

The bell was a sweet and beautiful sound to Michael as the tenth round came to a close. The smell of blood was set to turn his stomach, and he could probably produce a mouthful of it if asked. The swollen left eye was nearly closed; Michael saw two of his corner and opted to split the difference, aiming his body at the middle. The crowd rose to its feet and as the referee nudged the fighters to their respective corners. Michael looked up at Cortez; the champion was bleeding from the lip and holding his ribs. He nodded at Michael and smiled as much as his split lip would allow.

Michael nodded back.

Chapter Sixteen

Dutch worked quickly to stop the bleeding from the various spots on Michael's face. As soon as the kid sat down, he snapped the broken nose back into place and sealed his nostrils with cotton coated in petroleum jelly. He slapped the cold compress on his puffy left eye and held it there for a few seconds, then put the End-Swell in its place. Dutch pressed hard on the cold steel bar. A stream of bright red blood trickled from the just under Michael's eye, gradually getting lighter in color before it stopped. Dutch quickly covered the spot with more ointment.

Michael knew all of this should hurt. He grunted as Dutch pushed and pulled at his nose, winced as sweat entered his cut as it was being ironed out. The cotton balls in his nose felt like the worst head cold he'd ever endured, and he could taste blood in the back of his throat. Michael knew there should be pain – discomfort, at least – but felt none of that. Dutch upended a water bottle on Michael's head, and he let some fall into his mouth. It was an impromptu cold shower, and it helped beat back some of the fatigue.

"This guy is way out of his depth," Dutch said in a reassuring tone. "These are championship rounds, he don't know nothing about that. You do. This is your time. Your show." Dutch turned towards Cortez's corner. "Look at him, Michael. You know what I see? He's tired. Desperate. He knows he don't got shit left on his punches and he's trying to put you down. He can't stand there and box toe-to-toe with you, not now, and he knows that. But you need to protect your nose." Dutch turned back around and gently eased the cotton balls out of Michael's nose. They were soaked in blood and snot, and a stubborn trail of congealed red slime connected them to his nose. Michael's first deep breath in nearly a minute hurt his ribs and sinus cavity, and was accompanied by the lingering acrid taste of blood in the back of his throat. He was breathing though, and that was enough.

"It'll hold up to maybe one good hit," Dutch said. "Any more than that and it'll come loose, and I might not be able to stop the blood this time. The nose, Mike, more than the ribs." Michael nodded that he understood. He looked across the ring to Cortez's corner. His handlers helped him to his feet and massaged his shoulders.

"Okay, kid, it's show time!" Dutch slipped Michael's mouthpiece back into his mouth and helped him to his feet. Michael inhaled deeply through his nose twice. It still hurt, but the taste of blood wasn't as strong.

"Seconds out!" the ref called as Dutch was sliding out of the ring. Michael strode to the center of the ring and touched gloves with Cortez just as the bell rang to start the round.

☆ ☆ ☆

The week before…

Dutch wasn't exactly the trusting type.

It's why he always trained Michael by himself, why he never used cut men or corner men, and why he and Michael were by themselves preparing for the flight to Las Vegas. It was one of the things Michael loved about the man; it was never about whether he was paranoid, just whether he was paranoid enough. So it came as no surprise to Michael when, an hour before they had to leave the gym for the airport, Dutch voiced a concern.

"I'm not so sure this is such a great idea," he said.

"Flying coach?" Michael smiled.

"Don't be stupid. This plan, if that's what you want to call it. I don't like it."

"You pick now to tell me this?" Michael said. "I mean, we've been training for the last eight weeks."

"I'm not sure that's enough time, not for a title fight. Not for Cortez." Dutch sat on a stool outside the training ring. "Say what you will about the man, but he's champion for a reason. The man is a nightmare, and that's in a fight where you're supposed to have a chance." Dutch heaved a sigh and shook his head. "Look, I'm in this either way, but I can't let you go out there without telling you this is a bad idea. Can you tell me you think you can beat Cortez?"

Michael smiled and unzipped the front pocket of his roller suitcase. He reached in and pulled out a long, manila envelope with a rectangular bulge. "I'm betting on it," he said as he tossed the envelope towards Dutch. It landed with a slap and skidded on the Basement's cold concrete floor until it hit Dutch's shoe.

Dutch bent over and picked it up. His mouth hung open as he slid his hand inside the envelope. The brick in the envelope was ten stacks of hundred dollar bills, banded in five thousand-stacks. Fifty grand. Dutch stared at the money silent and slack-jawed. "Are. You. Crazy?" he said, slowly and quietly. "Are you fucking insane? Tell me this isn't Dante's money. Please tell me." Michael shrugged and Dutch grabbed at his chest with his left hand. "Jesus H. Christ," he panted. "What are you thinking? You're gonna gamble this money? To do what? Are you trying to get yourself killed?"

"Does it matter?" Michael said. "I don't think it does. Not really. I got bigger fish to fry. I'm trying to get free. I'm trying to set my kid up so she can do stuff I never thought to. I'm trying to pay you back for... well, for everything."

"This isn't the way to do it," Dutch said. "Gambling this money..."

Michael raised his hand to silence the old man. "I'm trying to be a man," he said solemnly. "So maybe this isn't the way you would have picked for it to happen. Not sure I would have gone this road either, given a choice. We deal with what we deal with."

Dutch stared down at the money, the stacks fanned out like a poker hand. "Jesus. I've never seen this much cash at once before. I didn't expect it to be so heavy." He inhaled a deep whiff of the money and smiled.

"Smell good, don't it," Michael said with a smile.

"What about Cortez?" Dutch said, looking up from the money. He stuffed it back in the envelope and sealed it. "I mean, either Cortez knows this fight is supposed to be a throw and he kills you out there, or he's expecting it to be straight-up, and he kills you out there."

Michael smiled broadly and took the money from Dutch. "Let me worry about Cortez," he said.

Halfway through the 11th round, Cortez was visibly tired and mouth breathing, but he still managed to double up on the jabs to the body. Michael got his arms in front of his midsection and turned his body to deflect the incoming shots. They were coming slowly enough that he saw them coming, but Michael was tired too, and was barely able to turn them back. After he deflected a weak-armed jab to the body, and another, a surprisingly quick right hand found its way to the clotting wound over Michael's eye, smudging the petroleum jelly bandage and causing a trickle of crimson to leak down the side of Michael's face. Michael stepped forward and gave Cortez a bear-hug of a clinch.

Fuck, he thought. *I can't believe he got that cut.*

The bear hug tightened as Cortez tried to wriggle free. Michael took two slow, deep breaths that fired off the pain receptors in his head and chest as his broken nose inhaled and his cracked ribs expanded.

I can't believe that weak-ass right hand got that cut.

The referee stepped in to separate them and took a glance at the cut over Michael's eye before waving the fight to continue. The constant ache from his injuries and the indignation of getting tagged with that weak right hand colored everything in Michael's field of vision red, and when the ref got out of the way, Michael stuck a left hand squarely on Cortez's nose and shuffled the champion back a step. Michael landed two quick jabs that snapped the champion's head back and when Cortez got his guard up, Michael went to the body and peppered the defense with four shots in rapid succession.

Cortez stepped back and took a breath through the mouth. He got his hands up around his head and tapped at Michael's body with the jab. When those shots were deflected, Cortez turned over a murderous right hand to Michael's jaw.

He saw double for a moment and stumbled back, trying to keep his head up. He tried to keep an eye on Cortez, who closed on him like a shark. Michael tried to step back, to stand up, to get his lower body to do anything on command, but gravity and dizziness conspired to aim him toward the canvas.

Quin Cortez's overhand right sent him there like a missile.

Michael snapped back to his senses as the ref counted three. He was face-down and near the ropes, looking across the ring at his corner. He saw four – no, two – of Dutch jumping wildly in the corner and waving his arms. He blinked twice and Dutch's twin disappeared, leaving only the one old man screaming maniacally. Michael was sure he was saying "Get up!" or some other urgent message. He braced himself on the canvas with his left hand and pulled his legs in under him.

Five. The ref said five and Michael wasn't sure what happened to four. He reached for the ropes with his right hand and hooked his glove around the second one up. He pushed with the left, pulled with the right and rose to one knee. He waited a breath to see if he was stable – he'd better be, the count was at six – before he let go of the rope.

He stayed on one knee until the eight count, the pushed up to his feet. The referee checked his hands and the cut in his eye, and when he was satisfied that Michael's brain wasn't too fried or that he wouldn't bleed to death, he waved them to continue. Michael tried to take a deep breath and stepped back into the fight.

Cortez circled from the outside again, stepping in to jab and back out before Michael had a chance to react. Cortez wasn't moving as fast as he was in the early rounds, and his footwork didn't look as sound. When he stepped in, his jab would be from flat feet, slowing him down for his escape. Michael got his guard up again, watching Cortez and waiting. Cortez lunged in, popped off two jabs and stepped back. Cortez circled another couple of steps, jumped in the same way, and stepped back.

Cortez stepped back in just as the ten-second warning went off, and as he fired off the jab, Michael stepped to the side. A left hook to the chest and a straight right to the mouth reopened his cut lip and sent the champion spiraling to the canvas.

The crowd noise and tinnitus made it nearly impossible for Michael to hear the referee count, but it didn't matter. He knew that Cortez wouldn't stay down, that Cortez would beat the count and that this fight was going to go to a twelfth and final round. As the champion rose to his feet, his face as bloody and sweat-soaked, Michael was never happier to be right.

Chapter Seventeen

The night before...

"Weighing in first," the ring announcer said, his voice booming through the speakers in the ballroom at the MGM Grand. Photographers from various news outlets immediately aimed their cameras to the announcer's right where, in front of a billboard sized promotion shot, stood Michael Dane and Dutch. "With a professional record of twenty-two wins and three losses and with nineteen coming by way of knockout, fighting out of the Dewey Street Gym in Brooklyn, New York, the number one contender to the International Boxing Federation's World Light-Heavyweight Championship, the challenger, Michael, 'the Panther,' Dane!"

Michael quickly yanked off his sweatpants and his Dewey Street Gym T-Shirt and handed them off to Dutch. He drew a couple of shrieks from the female fans in attendance as he stepped onto the electronic scale. He shifted his weight between his legs until he was balanced and comfortable, allowing the readout to settle one number.

"Michael Dane weighs in tonight at..." The ring announcer paused to get a good look at the bright red digital readout. "One hundred seventy-one and three-quarter pounds!" Flashbulbs popped and Michael did the obligatory five-second flex for the cameras. He glanced out to the crowd and saw Dante Alexander, with Boone to his right and Cortez's manager/promoter, Miguel Castillo to his left, sitting two rows behind the press. Dante and Miguel talked discreetly to one another, and when Dante looked up, he gave a nod in Michael's direction. Michael turned to his left and walked toward Dutch.

"Fucking hate that asshole," he mumbled to Dutch under his breath.

"And now, weighing in next," the ring announcer said as the small crowd began to percolate. Whistling and shrieking echoed throughout the ballroom and the atmosphere became thick with anticipation. Quin Cortez entered from the left side of the stage to a chorus of high-pitched squeals and cheers, followed by his trainer and his cut man. He was shirtless on arrival, showing off his chiseled physique to the admirers in the crowd. His trainer walked with the championship belt, cradled in his arms as if it were his newborn child. He adjusted the belt so that the large gold medallions that adorned it were facing the crowd. "Hailing from Miami, by way of Santo Domingo in the Dominican Republic, he is undefeated in his professional career with twenty wins and eighteen by way of knockout, he is the reigning and defending International Boxing Federation Light-Heavyweight champion." The ring announcer paused for effect, hamming up the drama as the crowd grew more excited. "'El Conquistador,' Quin Cortez!"

Cortez walked up to the scale and made a show of tearing off his break-away pants, revealing briefs in the color of the Dominican flag. He twirled for the women in attendance, who squealed with adolescent joy when they saw the single white Dominican star on his butt. When he was done toying with the crowd he stepped onto the scale and after a moment of being still, the digital readout settled on a number that the ring announcer double checked before getting on the microphone.

"Quin Cortez weighs in tonight at an even one hundred and seventy pounds." Cortez posed on the scale as even more flashbulbs went off, pointing out to the crowd in the direction of some of the camera. Security for the event and personnel from the pay-per-view herded Michael towards Cortez for some publicity shots.

"Okay, fight pose," one photographer said. The two men stood a quarter-step from each other, Michael's left fist at Cortez's chin, and the champion's right fist on Michael's chin.

"Get used to this," Cortez mumbled under his breath as cameras clicked and whirred around them.

The two men were turned face-to-face and Michael found himself uncomfortably close to the Champ. Michael heard Cortez breathe, felt hot carbon dioxide exhaled onto his face and smelled the garlic on Cortez's breath. He saw Quin Cortez narrow his gaze to a squint. Michael stayed back on his heels; he was ready at a moment's notice to step back from the garlic death mist escaping Cortez's mouth and torching his eyebrows.

"Do you ever think to brush before one of these things?" Michael said.

"Shut up, chump," Cortez shot back. "Enjoy these breaths, because you're not getting many more of them."

Michael smiled and looked over at Cortez's trainer, who still held the title belt in his arms like an infant. "Tell your boy to keep that warm for me," he said. "You won't be needing that anymore."

"Hey, *maricon*," Cortez said, slapping Michael's face. "How about you worry about me right here."

Michael immediately shoved Cortez back, hard as the crowd in attendance suddenly went from politely excited to collectively rooting. "Fuck you," he growled, instinctively releasing the tension in his arms and planting his feet. The "fight-or-flight" switch in Michael's head was definitely stuck at fight, and Cortez only stumbled back a step or two before he leaned towards Michael. Security stepped in quickly and separated the two men.

Cortez resisted against the three burly guards as they guided him out of the room. "They won't be here to save you, punk," he shouted from across the room.

Michael was more passive as he was led away. He got his hands free and up in the air. His right forefinger tapped his left wrist, where his watch would be. "Tick-tock," he shouted. "Your time's running out, Cortez! See you tomorrow!"

Dutch cleaned up the trickle of blood above Michael's eye with a cotton swab and resealed the wound with a dab of ointment. The blood clotted behind the clear gel and turned it pink. He went on to press down on a small mouse that had formed on Michael's cheek with the end-swell, and with his free hand, coaxed the mouth guard from his fighter's mouth. He dropped the steel bar after a few seconds and grabbed a bottle of water. He doused the mouthpiece with half the bottle and dumped the other half over Michael's head.

The cold water snapped Michael out of his trance. The knockdown last round and the thirty seconds afterwards was a blur and had stunted his ability to concentrate. Quite frankly, he couldn't remember how exactly he got to the corner. His eyes shot over to Dutch as he worked dutifully on cleaning the mouth guard. Michael quickly ran his tongue over the back of his teeth and the roof of his mouth. Sure enough, he tasted the metallic tang of blood, probably from his broken nose. His nose still hurt, but not like earlier; either the pain was fading, or he had just gotten used to it. He looked at Dutch's face, focused on his mouth, expecting to hear some kind of sage advice for the final round about how he should dig deep into whatever reserves he had left or some tip he had gleaned from watching Cortez fight for eleven rounds. Instead, Dutch was silent, mouth not moving, as he went about the business of getting Michael cleaned up and ready for the final round.

Dutch grabbed a squirt bottle filled with water and aimed it at his tired fighter's mouth. Michael opened and allowed the short stream to rinse his mouth clean of blood. He swished it around, spit a pink spurt into the bucket on his right, and opened his mouth for another blast of water to swallow. He opened his mouth one more time, and Dutch slid the mouth piece in.

The ref called "Seconds out!" and the crowd noise quickly and steadily rose to deafening. Michael watched Cortez get up slowly and bounce on the balls of his feet in the corner. Michael grabbed the ropes for leverage and got himself up. Dutch stepped in front of him and grabbed his shoulder, leveling his eye with his pupil's.

"I'm proud of you," Dutch said, giving Michael two playful slaps to the face. With that, he got out of the way, ducked out of the ring and took all his stuff with him.

A smile slowly broke out over Michael's face as he approached his opponent in the center ring. The bell was barely audible above the noise level of the crowd, waiting with heightened anticipation of the final round. Alternating chants for Quin Cortez and Michael Dane rained down on them, showing appreciation for a legendary night, a title fight worthy of each and every hard-fought round. Michael looked up to the skybox, to where the orange light of Dante's cigar had been flickering for the last 45 minutes. The cigar light was not there and the seat was probably now empty. Dante was gone.

Michael turned his attention back to Cortez. "I hope your boy Castillo comes through on his promise," he said. Michael held out his glove, and with a smile, Cortez touched it.

"Let's make history," the Champ said as the bell rung to start round 12.

☆ ☆ ☆

The night before...

It was 2:00 in the morning and Michael couldn't sleep. His insomnia was powered by the same nervous energy that would lead most people staying at the MGM Grand to blow their life's savings at the casino. There was something in the marble, the steel, the concrete of the building that seemed to generate and amplify that energy. Michael knew that feeling all too well. It was the same itch that drove him to do very stupid things in his youth. It had led him to a point where he owed money to all the wrong people, and ultimately brought him here, fittingly, to Las Vegas, hours away from the fight of his life. The fifty thousand dollars in his luggage called to him. Old, familiar thoughts of blackjack and fast-paced betting briefly teased the back of his mind. He had to move.

He dropped to the floor and rattled off fifty pushups.

It was a trick he learned in prison, when the confinement started to mess with his head. Those long nights when he couldn't see anything in the darkness, and couldn't hear anything but faint snoring somewhere in the complex, he would silently roll out of bed and do pushups. Or crunches. Some nights he would alternate between both for hours. It was like putting ointment on an itch; it would stop the sensation for a while, but a few hours later, it would wake you up again just as intense as it was before.

At 2:45 the knock at the door he was expecting finally came. By then, he was halfway through his fourth set of crunches, already having logged one hundred and fifty. He grunted as he got to his feet staggered over to the door, slightly out of breath. After a quick check of the peephole, he opened for Quin Cortez. They stared at each other for a very long ten seconds.

"It's about damn time," Michael said as he turned around and pushed the door open wide enough for Quin to enter. The door whooshed as it swung shut, and the counterweights in the door hinges slowed it enough that it closed with a soft click.

"I had to make sure I wasn't being followed," the other man said. His demeanor seemed quite different than at the weigh-in; gone was that cocky, larger-than-life attitude he wore in the ring. He almost seemed… smaller, which was weird considering at five-foot-nine, he wasn't that big to begin with. He walked over to the mini-bar across the room and pulled out a small bottle of vodka. He quickly cracked it open and drained it dry, coughing as the vile alcohol burned its way down his throat. "Can I ask you something?" he said, leaning against the mini-bar. "Why in the hell are you shirtless and sweaty? Who were you expecting, exactly?"

Michael looked over to the couch in the living room portion of the suite and realized he had forgotten to put his shirt back on. He walked over and quickly replaced the garment. "This make you feel better?" he said.

"Much," Quin replied, flicking the bottle over to the blue recycling bin ten feet across from him.

"So?" Michael said. "Is your boy Castillo gonna look out for me or what? I mean, I did put him on to all of this happening, how Dante was trying to fuck him."

"Yeah, yeah, but I'm not so sure he's my boy anymore. Dude's trying to sell my contract out from under me? That's fucked up."

Michael nodded. "So it's all good? Selena's gonna be protected?"

"Dante won't be able to get close to her. Miguel Castillo is a well-connected motherfucker. He knows a lot of people, and a lot

of people owe him favors. Friends in high and low places, I guess."
Michael breathed a heavy sigh of relief. "I got a question though,"
Quin said. "When you came to me with this, why didn't you try
to get something out of this for yourself? Maybe, to survive the
night without throwing the fight?"

Michael stared at the ground as he thought back to the initial
phone conversation they had four weeks prior.

"Don't feed me that nonsense, you know exactly who I am,"
he had said to the champion.

"What do you want?" Cortez's voice was angry, confrontational.
The few times they had met before they exchanged very little in
the way of conversation.

"We need to talk. Your contract's being sold from under you.
Did you know that?"

"Sold?" Cortez asked. "The hell you mean, sold? To who?"

"Dante Alexander. And it's being low-balled because your
managers don't think you can beat me. Well, that and because
you're a crap draw as a champion." Michael smiled and there was
a long moment of silence on the other end. "Still there?"

"You still haven't told me what you want."

Michael ran down the situation as quickly as he could; how
the sale was being done with the idea that Cortez was barely
bookable as a champion, and since his team didn't think he could
win, he would be a liability. He talked about Dante's plan to
throw the fight, so he could acquire the contract of a champion
at a cut-rate price. "What I want," he finally said, "is a favor from
Miguel Castillo."

The weeks that passed had the two of them in fairly constant
contact, with Quin Cortez acting as the reluctant go-between
for Michael Dane and Miguel Castillo. Castillo and Cortez's
relationship was shattered, but they put that aside for the sake
of putting on a good fight and getting back at Dante. Michael

agreed that if he could stay in the fight past the sixth round, Castillo would keep Selena out of danger without ever showing his face around her, and in turn, Castillo would hire Dutch as Quin Cortez's new trainer.

"Yo, Mike, you still here?"

Michael's mind snapped back to the hotel room. "Yeah. I never asked for anything because all I want is a fair fight."

A slow smile broke out over Quin Cortez's face. "I get it," he said with a small chuckle. "Rest up," he said as he headed to the door. He grabbed the handle and paused a moment. "Piece of advice," he said. "A fight this big, your nerves will kill you long before I do. Take a shot of something. It'll make your stomach feel rotten and full of butterflies, but once the adrenaline gets going, you'll be good." Having said his piece, Quin Cortez turned the door handle and walked out.

The bell sounded for the final round and an excited, but emotionally weary crowd started a standing ovation. Cortez bounced around, circling Michael on the outside of his range. The tactic was different this time, though. The previous rounds and the pounding he took to his midsection made the champion unable to scoot out of the way of Michael's jab; the first two landed right on his chest, just beneath his collar bone. Michael grunted with each jab he threw, putting everything he could spare behind them. After those two shots, it was all Cortez could do to tuck his head to his chin and get his arms across his body. He bent over slightly to minimize the target.

With Cortez protecting his body so closely, his head was exposed and Michael made him pay for it with a quick jab-hook from the left hand. He leaned into the hook for more emphasis, and the sound of leather hitting skin sounded like a solid, open-handed slap. Cortez backed up another two steps, coming out of his shell and breathing a second. He motioned for Michael to come towards him with his fists. Michael approached with caution, leading with a jab to the body that Cortez didn't even try to avoid. He got his hands back and swayed back and forth while Cortez danced, scoring another, more confident jab that the champ made no effort to avoid.

"Don't let him bait you," Michael faintly heard Dutch say, right before he planted his foot and leaned into an overhand right aimed directly at the top of Cortez's nose. At the last second Cortez leaned back and Michael was left off-balance, his weight shifted forward. Cortez slipped in a short left uppercut and followed it up with a surprisingly strong right hook, bringing the crowd to their feet in anticipation of a knockdown. Michael shook off the weakened blows as he hopped back two steps to regain his bearings.

Michael pounded his fists together and reset his attack, staying back and peppering Cortez's defense from the outside. Cortez was visibly gassed and not nearly as speedy as he was in the early rounds, so Michael scored four solid body shots from the outside before Cortez could scamper out of range. The champ shook his head and snorted loudly as he narrowed his eyes at his opponent. Michael advanced and landed one more jab before the champion lunged at him, getting inside Michael's range and landing a couple of power shots inside.

Michael deflected most of the incoming blows to his midsection with body movement, weaving himself out of harm's way. The incoming shots slowed down some as fatigue compromised Cortez's technique, and Michael dropped a short-armed hook to the champion's jaw and followed it up with a stiff left jab and a straight right. The crowd was riled up as he tapped at the champ's head with a jab, then another, and followed it up with an overhand right that found a landed square on Cortez's forehead.

The champion staggered but stayed upright. He didn't waste a second getting back in the fight, throwing big sweeping hooks to Michael's head. One landed flush on the left side of the challenger's face, turning his head and making him step back. Michael charged right back into the fray, landing another stiff left jab and left hook, then turning over the overhand right. He figured Dutch would probably kill him for going toe-to-toe with Cortez like this.

The crowd's excitement nearly drowned out the ten-second warning, and both fighters went after each other with the gusto of a feeding frenzy in a shark tank, and when the bell rang, the referee stepped between them to signal that it was over, and both men pounded each other's fists in the middle of the ring. The crowd gave them a standing ovation, and neither fighter could hide the smiles from their battered, bruised faces.

Chapter Eighteen

The night before...

Michael only had a couple of things to do after Quin Cortez left the suite. He had to call his bookie, Lenny, a number he hadn't used since he was released from prison. Lenny was a greasy, godless bastard who would take bets on almost anything, and indulged in all manner of unsavory vices. Without a doubt, the man would be up at this time of night, but he could wait.

Michael flipped through his contact list to Selena's name. She was due any day, now, he had given her an emergency cell phone for when she went into labor pre-programmed with him on speed dial. He was hoping it would have happened before tonight.

He paced around the foyer of the suite as the phone rang and anxiously waited for her to pick up.

"Mmmnnyello?" came the groggy, raspy response. Something about the timbre of her voice early in the morning always drove him wild.

"Hey," he said softly, "did I wake you?"

"No, no. This kid of yours won't let me sleep much anymore. God, I just wish she'd make up her mind to get out of me already." They laughed, and Michael couldn't remember the last time they had a relaxed laugh like that. "It's okay though. Sun's coming out, so I should be getting up anyway. What time is it there?"

Michael looked over at the ornate wall clock. "Quarter after five," he said, shaking his head and massaging the bridge of his nose. "That makes it just after seven there. It's way early for you to be up."

"Whatever. I wanted to wake up early and call you anyway." She giggled a bit. "Your daughter has something to say." The background noise on the other end of the phone went dead as Michael assumed she pressed the phone against her belly. Michael heard nothing for a moment, then something that sounded like the ocean, like putting a conch shell against your ear. Very shortly after that, the limited background noise came back up. "Did you hear that?" Selena said excitedly. "She kicked! I told her to say hi to Daddy and she kicked!"

"That's…" He wanted to say it was the silliest thing he'd ever heard of, or that he didn't hear anything. But his daughter just kicked. Michael felt a smile push its way through to his face, and he almost forgot about what was in store for the rest of the day. "That's so freakin' cool!" he said.

"I think she's saying good luck," Selena said. "I'm just going to tell you to kick his ass." They laughed again for a moment, and a silence fell over them.

"So what happens now?" Michael asked. "What happens after the fight?"

"I don't know," she said. "Things are so good right now. I have you, I'm having this baby. It almost seems like a family."

"A family," Michael said. "Never had one of those before."

"Well, there's one here if you want it, waiting for you when you come back."

Michael wanted to tell her, right then and there, that there was a very good chance he wasn't coming back. That he had made choices that would make a coming back just not an option. "After this fight," he said and paused to catch his breath. He couldn't do that to her. "After this fight," he started again, "things are gonna be even better."

"Really?" she replied, and Michael felt the bottom of his stomach drop.

"I'm gonna make sure you and the baby will have everything," he said. "The two of you, my girls, you're gonna be so happy. I'm gonna make sure you get everything you ever wanted. It's gonna be…"

"Michael, I love you."

Whoomp! The words hit like a punch to his gut. It made him quickly nauseous and he had a hard time fighting back the urge to vomit. He froze on the phone, open-mouthed, unable to move, breathe, or blink.

Selena giggled. "It's okay, you know," she said. "I know it's a big thing to spring on you, especially on the phone, especially right before your fight, but it's the first time I've ever said it to you and meant it. You don't have to say it back, but I just wanted you to know that I love you with all my heart."

The words again were caught in Michael's throat, and the choking made him tear up. He coughed twice and sniffled, then brushed away a stray tear that snaked its way out of his tightly shut eyelids. His knees shook violently and he leaned against the wall to brace himself.

"I'm gonna go," she said. "Talk soon?"

"Okay," Michael said. "I love you too."

Through the phone, he felt her smile. "Okay. We'll talk soon." And she hung up.

Michael leaned against the wall and let the tears roll down his face. A few minutes passed – or maybe a few hours, as the next time he looked up the bright eastern sunrise set the sky ablaze

- Michael made his way over to the desk in the bedroom portion of the suite. He opened the drawer and pulled out a pen and a notepad of hotel stationary, and started to write.

✶ ✶ ✶

The two fighters hugged in the center of the ring, surrounded by trainers and entourages, like old friends who hadn't seen each other in a long time. In the minute since the final bell went off, the crowd deluged the two fighters with affection and applause and alternating chants for Michael Dane and Quin Cortez rained down from every section of the crowd. No matter who the chants were for, though, everyone in attendance knew they'd just seen something very special.

"Good fight," Cortez said breathily, patting Michael on the back of his head. "Anytime you want to do that again, it's on."

Michael nodded and smiled as much as his battered face would let him. "No doubt," he panted, with the suspicious feeling like he would fall over. The two men broke the hug and when the referee came and grabbed them both by the wrist. The ring announcer walked up to both of them and congratulated them on a great fight just as he was handed a slip of paper. Michael assumed it was the judges' scores.

"Here we go, kid," Dutch said as he stood on Michael's right hand side. "The whole sum of your life, down to the numbers on that sheet."

The ring announcer looked over the scores and nodded to the young man who brought them over. He grabbed the microphone that was lowered into the ring and cleared his throat. "Ladies and Gentlemen," he said, immediately silencing the crowd. "I have received the judges' scores, but first a round of applause for these two incredible gladiators and the amazing show they just put on!"

The crowd immediately restarted their cheering and applause, once again alternating chants for Michael and Quin. The ring announcer put up his right hand and the crowd again quieted. "And now for the judges' decision. Judge Simon Barstow scores this fight 95 to 92; Judge Andrew Scoleri scores this fight 95 to 96; and Judge Scott Griffin scores this fight 94 to 96 for the winner by split decision…"

The ring announcer paused for a moment, and Michael saw his life flash before his eyes. Every fight he had, every decision he made played before him like a subliminal blooper reel at triple the speed. He thought of the people who always claimed to see their lives flash before their eyes during a near-death experience and realized they must have been judged at that moment. Michael's entire life' worth hung in the expansive seconds of silence before the official announcement. The crowd was still split on their support, with people in the crowd still chanting both fighters' names almost as if dueling. As the call-response chants of "Michael Dane! Quin Cortez!" went on, they escalated in volume to a near fever pitch.

"… and the NEW…"

Half the crowd erupted in a chorus of cheers as Michael's legs finally gave, fatigue and emotion sending him to the canvas. He sat on the mat, stunned, by the three little words he'd just heard. A tear rolled down his cheek and a smile nearly split his battered face in half.

"… IBF Light-Heavyweight Champion of the World, 'the Panther,' Michael Dane!"

Dutch dropped to his knees and hugged his protégé; both men were tearful on the mat and laughed uncontrollably. The referee presented the belt to Michael, and Dutch helped him to his feet to receive it. Quin Cortez came over and gave Michael a handshake and a hug. "Congratulations," the former champion said with a smile and a nod. "I'm coming back for that title."

Michael laughed and smiled back, still teary and still laughing. He walked over to the corner of the ring and climbed up two of the ropes. He raised his arm and was buffeted by the cheers from the capacity crowd. His movements were restricted by the pain in his ribs, but in those moments he was in a world beyond pain. He raised the orange-and-gold belt above his head and pointed at a camera, then tapped the tattoo on his chest twice and mouthed "I love you."

And as Dutch helped him down from the ropes, somewhere in the back of Michael's consciousness he heard Selena say she loved him back.

Chapter Nineteen

The halogen floodlights they used in the press room made Michael's eyes hurt despite the dark sunglasses he wore to hide the bruising. He squinted, trying to see the reporters through the onslaught of glaring light, but the act made his temples throb. He felt lightheaded and queasy, likely from dehydration and fatigue and the countless punches he took to the head. Then, of course, there was the fact that he'd won the fight clean and was now the reigning light-heavyweight champion of the world.

In any event, he was drained and groggy and on top of the world.

He gripped the championship belt that was slung across his shoulder. The gaudy orange leather was stiff, the gold plates heavier than he expected it to be. Every time it touched his ribcage, pain would shoot up the left side of his body, stealing his breath along the way. There was no way he was going to make it out of there under his own power.

The post-fight interviews were a blur of questions and answers: first Cortez's trainer got up and praised the job Dutch did with Michael in getting ready for the fight, how when they heard he was coming back to Michael's camp they had to change the game plan. Cortez got up and said that on that night, the better man won. He praised the new champion, thanked him for a career defining fight, and promised that now that he'd suffered his first loss—his "cherry popped," as he so eloquently put it—he had nothing left to fear, so the division had best look out. He then turned toward the new champion, and with a smirk that threatened to split his lip again, he pointed at Michael and said, "Including you."

Michael couldn't help but laugh. That guy knew how to work a crowd.

Dutch was next at the podium. He praised Quin Cortez and his handlers for the opportunity to put on such a great show. Then, through tightly gnashed teeth, he thanked Dante Alexander and Inferno Entertainment for setting the whole thing up. He went on for another moment or two, wearing his best fake smile when talking about Dante.

Finally, Michael limped up to the podium with the championship belt draped over his shoulder. He decided he liked the feel of it there, broken rib or not, and would never wear it around his waist. He thanked Cortez and Miguel Castillo for finally allowing him the chance to compete. He mentioned that Quin Cortez had been an amazing champion and representative of the division and sport, and expressed his hope that he could be half as good as that. He thought about thanking Dante and Inferno Entertainment for setting up the fight. Thankfully a reporter in the front row interrupted with a question.

"So Michael, after losing two years of your career to prison, to being a slim favorite to win this fight, where does this rank in terms of success for you?"

Michael cracked a smile through the pain of his ribs. "Oh, yeah," he said. "Oh yeah. Huge success. I mean, this goes beyond just a win. This is…" He stopped and cocked his head to think about it. A single tear rolled down his cheek. "This is that big victory I'll be thinking about for the rest of my life."

He brushed the tear away as he pointed to another reporter. "So, Michael, Quin just threw down the gauntlet for a rematch." "Are you kidding me?" he said, cutting the reporter off mid thought. A chuckle rippled through the room. "I got a broken rib, a broken nose, my eye's busted open. I'm headed to the hospital after this! I think he's in the ambulance right next to me! If we survive the night, then maybe we can talk about a rematch." The room burst into laughter.

Dutch helped Michael back to the locker room to wait for the ring doctor to arrive. It was standard after every fight to get a quick checkup before being released, especially in a fight where both fighters were beaten so badly. The ring doctor simply patched them up until they could get through the interviews. Michael still wore the championship belt over his shoulder. He sat on the bench with his back to the wall as the doctor tended to his face. The cut above his eye had stopped bleeding, thanks in large part to Dutch's expert care during the fight, and the one on his cheek looked worse than it actually was. The overall swelling on his face had already started to go down. He was handed a couple of Percocet tablets and told that the paramedics would be there soon to take him to the ER to treat him for the probable concussion.

Dutch sat next to him and put a hand on his shoulder. "You good, kid?" he asked, smiling as wide as Michael had ever seen.

Michael smiled back and slapped the big gold plate on his new title belt. "I'm good," he said. He gently slipped his shoulder out from under the belt and handed it to his mentor. "Hold on to this for me," he said. "I don't want to lose track of it at the hospital."

Dutch smiled and laughed as he took the belt from Michael. His hands shook as he picked up the heavy strap, and he was a bit dazzled by the shiny gold ornaments. He laughed and forced back a tear. "We did it," he said, finally. "Your dad would be proud of us."

Michael smiled. "Aren't you?"

Dutch paused for a moment. He looked up at his pupil and thought briefly about all they had been through over the years. He helped the boy become a man. He was as much the boy's father as Stephen Dane. Maybe more. "I guess I am," Dutch said softly, the tear breaking through his shut eyelids.

There was a knock on the locker room door and two EMT's entered the locker room – one tall and thin, the other short and stocky, and neither one looking like they could carry Michael if he needed it. "Mr. Dane?" the tall one said. "Come with us please."

Michael got to his feet, steadied himself on his legs, and walked over to the two men. "Don't forget to clean out my locker, Dutch," he said as he walked out.

For a few long minutes after the paramedics took Michael away, Dutch sat on the bench in that locker room and stared at the belt, feeling the stiff orange leather and the weight of the gold plates. "Finally," he mumbled to himself. "After all this time." He smiled and set it down and walked across the room to Michael's locker. His gym bag was already packed and zipped, and on top of it was a manila envelope. He cocked his head to the side and picked it up. A Post-It note was affixed to the front.

Hope your next fighter is less of a pain in the ass.

Dutch's fingers trembled as he opened the envelope. Inside was a betting ticket with his name on it and a Las Vegas phone number for Lenny Beck. It took a second for the old man to place the name. Michael's old bookie. A chill crept up Dutch's spine as he perused the rest of the envelope's contents: a note to Dutch and a little white envelope addressed "To My Little Fighter on her 18th Birthday."

Dutch felt acid burn his throat as he read the note. "Please make sure half the fight purse goes to Selena and the other half goes to my kid. The bet is for you." A dim light went off from inside the side pocket of his gym bag along with the sound of an air-raid siren. Dutch reached inside and grabbed the cell phone. The name on the caller ID read "SHE'S COMING!"

He stumbled back across the room and slumped back onto the bench. There was uneasiness in his stomach, like dancing girls doing a salsa. He looked at the note, glanced over at the belt and shook his head.

"You son of a bitch," was all Dutch could manage to say. Tears streaked down his face.

The ride to the hospital was always Michael's favorite part after a fight. The back of an ambulance was so much roomier than the back of a limo, and the service was better. So were the drugs. He laid flat on the gurney and dozed a moment, letting the turns on the street rock his swimming head to sleep. Concussions gave the worst hangovers.

The nearest hospital was ten minutes away, but less than five minutes into the ride the ambulance stopped abruptly. Outside, Michael heard muffled voices, then two muffled pops, like popcorn in a bag. The back of the ambulance creaked open slowly, and two men stood at the opening. Their faces were washed out by the painkillers in Michael's system and the bright lights of the city behind them, but Michael knew who they were.

He sighed. "Dante. Boone."

Dante stepped into the back of the ambulance and sat beside Michael's gurney. Boone stepped in behind him and the back of the van sunk four inches. The bigger man's steady breathing quickly filled the cramped ambulance with the distinct fetid odor of tooth decay and rotting meat and it made Michael cough painfully.

And then Dante lit a cigar.

"That was a good fight," Dante said grudgingly. He blew smoke rings out the back of the ambulance. "You may not believe this, but I *am* proud of you." Michael ignored him and rolled his head away. "I knew you had *it*," he continued. "You had that thing in you that makes people do great things. I knew you would be a stud in this sport at the right time. Maybe I was wrong about the timing, but…" Dante's voice trailed off and puffed on his cigar. He sighed deeply as he let out a cloud of gray smoke. "You cost me a lot of money tonight, Mike. I like you, but…"

"If you're going to kill me," Michael interrupted, "then get on with it. I don't have all night."

Dante looked at Michael for a moment. "I always liked you," he said with a smile. He stood up and stepped out of the ambulance, giving Boone a nod as he walked out. Boone produced one of his gold plated 9mm handguns and pointed it at Michael.

Michael saw the muzzle of the weapon flash twice, but he only heard the gun pop once. The second flash was accompanied by a loud ringing noise. Michael couldn't hear himself gasp.

Then darkness.

Epilogue

She had come to really hate birthdays.

It wasn't as if she didn't like the things that came with birthdays -- the presents, the attention, more presents -- she just wasn't a fan of the day itself. On her fifth birthday, she asked her mom why she didn't have a dad. Her mother did the absolute worst thing a parent could do.

She told the truth; her dad died on the day she was born.

The girl's mother had told her several stories as to what kind of man her father was: kind, loving, protective and loyal. How he tried at every turn to be a better man, and how, in her opinion, succeeded. By the time she was seven, she realized that there was a good chance her mother made these stories up to not speak ill of the dead. Kayla very often found herself angry and fixated on fighting. She was suspended several times in middle school before her mother taught her to re-channel that energy into her schoolwork. "Your father would have wanted that," she said, and that was all it took.

As the girl got older, she did her research. Her father was a boxer, as was his father (which explained her athletic stature and short temper), and a champion. He was the light heavyweight champion of the world when he died. He had done some time for a weapons charge, which she figured accounted for her penchant for meeting disappointing boyfriends. She took her search further, asking questions around the sport. Her father was some kind of urban legend.

Michael Dane was one tough bastard, one guy would say.

He could take a punch as good as he gave.

He had a heart and chin of steel.

By the time she was fifteen, Kayla Dane turned finding information on her father into an obsession. Where most girls her age would have posters of boy bands or teen stars on their bedroom walls, hers were adorned with old newspaper clippings of her father. She had little to no interest in music videos, but she combed through ESPN's Classic Fights whenever she could, paying special attention to her dad's fights.

Her mother's continued insistence that she focus some of that obsession on school is what eventually drove her to earning a free ride at an Ivy League school, and at the end of the summer, that's where she was headed. However, today was her eighteenth birthday, and for the eighteenth time, she would watch her mother die a little inside at the memory that her highest high and lowest low happened on the same day.

Kayla opted to do a small dinner with her mother this year in lieu of inviting a bunch of people from school over to her house for a party. Outside of the few classes she had with the kids in various social circles, she had nothing in common with those people. She certainly had no desire to have them in her home, spend time with them, and have them offer fake congratulations and birthday wishes in exchange for the opportunity to get drunk en masse at her house. All she wanted was a burger, and there was one place in SoHo that she wanted it from: Fanelli's, on the corner of Prince and Mercer. She could already taste it.

A knock on the door yanked her from her burger-laden daydream, and when Kayla opened it she saw an old man standing at the door. He was hunched forward slightly, shaking, and had a very nervous look on his face. Most of the hair on the top of his head was gone, and what was left was white. His dark skin showed few wrinkles or age lines, but Kayla figured he had to be pushing 80. When he caught sight of her however, his eyes -- one a healthy dark brown, the other clouded by cataracts – lit up with recognition.

"Michaela?" he said, in a creaky old voice that seemed more breathy than bassy. It was a voice that sounded like it had gone raw from shouting. "Michaela Andrea Dane?"

She stared at this odd old man. He seemed harmless enough, but he knew her name. How did he know her name?

The old man smiled at her, a tight-lipped smile that crunched the corners of his eyes. "Thank goodness you grew up to look like your mother instead of your old man."

Kayla raised an eyebrow at this and tilted her head towards the inside of the house. "Mom," she called. "There's a weird pervy old guy at the door."

Selena Arguella walked through the foyer to the door, stepping in front of her daughter and throwing the door open. She stared for a moment, then gasped. A smile spread across her face, and across the old man's. "Dutch," she said, a hint of music in her voice.

"Hello, Selena," Dutch replied, pulling the older woman in for a hug. "Time has been good to you. You haven't changed a bit." She was in her late forties, but still a very pretty Latin woman, and could very easily pass for Kayla's sister much to the girl's irritation. Her chest still defied gravity and though she always denied it, Kayla always thought her mom had work done. All in all, though, the two of them had done well and had a comfortable life.

The embrace was short and welcome, and Kayla took a less aggressive posture when she saw the creepy old guy knew her mom.

"Kayla, this is Terrence Masters." When Kayla asked silently why she should care, Selena continued. "He knew your father, and your grandfather. He was your father's trainer."

Kayla's hazel eyes – one of the genetic gifts she inherited from her mother – lit up as she extended her hand to shake Dutch's. "Call me Kayla," she said. "You should come on in."

They sat around a small round wooden table on the back deck, Dutch flanked by the two loves of his protégé's life: Selena on his left and Kayla on his right. He smiled and felt as if, for the first time in a long time, he was surrounded by family. "We met before, Micha… Kayla," he said. "It was on the day you were born, so I don't expect you to remember." Dutch smiled at his own bad joke. "I hopped on a plane to New York when your mom went into labor because your dad couldn't. I'm here today because it was the last wish of Michael Dane. I'm here because your father asked me to be. He was like a son to me, you know. I raised him like my own." Dutch reached inside his knapsack and produced a manila envelope. "Before he died, he asked me to give you this."

Kayla's breath became short and fast, sucking small mouthful of air through her lips. "You saw him before he died?" she asked. "Do you know what happened?"

Dutch looked over at Selena for a moment; she shut her eyes and put her head in her hands. "Your father had sustained some serious injuries during that title fight," he said. "But that's a story for another time. He left instructions through a letter. He wanted you to have this package."

Dutch handed her the manila envelope. It was thin in her hands, and almost seemed to be empty. She opened it and dumped out a crisp, new envelope from the bank and another envelope, white but yellowing, addressed "To my little fighter on her 18ᵗʰ birthday." Kayla's hands trembled as she held the envelope. She looked at her mother, then at Dutch, and back at the letter. "What is this?"

Dutch cupped one of her trembling hands in his own unsteady grasp. "Mike loved you," he said solemnly. "Both of you. That love made him grow up very quickly. He was a child in so many ways before he died. If that's what I think it is, then he became a man the night he wrote that."

Kayla's hands steadied themselves, and Dutch released the one he'd held. She studied the envelope -- the smooth feel of the paper on her fingertips, the careful, meticulous way all the letters were capitalized and the same height, even the way the corners, though slightly yellowed from aging, were still sharp. Great pains were taken to make sure she would get this. She was *supposed* to read this.

She reverently flipped the envelope over and slid her fingers over the seal. It was secure, but the glue was almost twenty years old, dry and brittle. She slipped her fingernail under the flap and gently separated it from the rest of the envelope. There was a letter inside, a few pages long, on white unlined stationery watermarked with the lion's head logo of the MGM Grand hotel. The paper itself had started to yellow with age. She unfolded the letter and looked at the dateline. She fought the urge to scream and pass out as a chill raced up her spine. It was October 31, eighteen years ago. The day she was born. The day he died.

Kayla quickly refolded the letter and slipped it back into its envelope. She took quick shallow breaths and trembled as she felt the tips of her toes tingle. She felt a chorus line doing the salsa in her stomach. She tried to focus on her breathing, in through her nose, out through her mouth. Selena got up quickly and disappeared into the refrigerator, producing a bottle of water. She handed it to Kayla, and tears streamed down both women's face. Kayla took the bottle and chugged a mouthful of the cold water.

"Maybe it would be best if you read that in private," Dutch said.

☆ ☆ ☆

Kayla retreated to her room without another word of thanks or farewell to Dutch. All that mattered was that manila envelope and its contents, the first and last message to her from her father. She dumped the two envelopes out onto the computer desk in the corner of her bedroom and turned on her desk lamp. Already open on her desk was another letter, one which she had been studying for almost a month – her acceptance letter to the University of Pennsylvania.

She brushed that letter to the side and studied the two envelopes before her. The one from the bank was pristine, looked like whatever was in it was put in earlier that day. She looked at the other envelope, the one with the letter in it and decided she didn't have it in her right that minute to read it. Just the thought of it made her heart attempt escape through her throat. She opened the bank envelope and found a statement of accounts.

Apparently, someone had started a trust fund for her that was initially worth $250,000, and accrued interest over the last eighteen years. She now had close to two million dollars in the bank, more than enough to pay for school. Her knees shook so much, she had to sit down.

It only took a moment to realize what had happened. Somehow, her father left this for her. It was the only thing that made sense. He'd left her mom a good sum of money, enough to get them a nice house in Queens and make sure they were comfortable. She hadn't wanted for anything. She slumped back in her desk chair and exhaled deeply. A tear rolled down her cheek as she smiled broadly and laughed.

That was a hell of a birthday gift.

She was about to run downstairs and celebrate with whomever was down there when she caught sight of the other envelope, the letter. She took a heavy sigh and grabbed it. The hairs on her arms stood up when she saw the date again. She swallowed the rising lump in her throat and started reading.

I don't even know your name.

My name is Michael Dane. I'm your father. If you're reading this then I'm dead. And of course you're reading this, because I know I'm going to die.

I saw you once. You were a black-and white image, a sonogram. That was the baby picture I had of you, and I showed you off frequently to my one and only friend. I saw you once and I fell in love immediately.

When I was young, I did some really stupid things, things that were far from the path my parents had wanted set for me. It was a dishonor to their memory, the things I did, and they led me here. The funny thing about here is that I have the opportunity to atone. I have the opportunity to give my life some meaning and maybe – just maybe – make you proud of me. I know this must be confusing to you. It's confusing to me. I want you to know that I died with my honor and self-respect intact, that I died doing the right thing.

I can only imagine the worlds you're about to discover, and offer nothing but regret for missing it. Knowing your mother, you're probably gifted with a temper, and knowing me you have the curse of stubbornness. I only hope the people in your life have directed you to find a positive way to channel that temper, that stubbornness. Let no one impede your goals. Don't sell out to anybody.

We were all meant to do great things, be it by accident or design. We are all given at least one opportunity to do one great thing. Don't let the opportunity pass you by when it presents itself. Only you will know when, only you will know what, but believe me when I say it will sing to you like nothing you'll ever hear. What I am doing, writing this letter, fighting this fight, this is what I'm supposed to be doing. This is that one opportunity. And even though taking it will mean I'm probably not walking away from this, I have no choice.

I don't know your name, never held you in my arms, but I love you with all my heart. Thank you for changing me. Now go do something great.

Your father,
Michael Andrew Dane.

☆ ☆ ☆

Kayla was careful not to let her tears land on the letter and smudge the ink and when she was done reading it, she read through it again. She had seen the tapes of his title fight, heard his voice in interviews and imagined it talking to her as she read the letter. She re-folded the pages and put them back in the envelope alongside the acceptance letter from the University of Pennsylvania.

It was clear to her what she had to do.

The odds were heavily against her mother understanding what she was doing. Dutch would probably throw up a bit of resistance as well, but they would have to learn to deal with it. She took the acceptance letter and ran over its matte finish with her fingertips, feeling the texture of the high-quality ink raised on the paper. She grabbed it at both ends and tore the letter in half, then in half again.

She knew who she was. She was a fighter, like her father and her father's father.

On the morning she was supposed to leave for Penn, she lightly packed a duffel bag full of workout clothes. She threw the bag in the backseat of the car and drove to Brooklyn.

She paced nervously outside the Dewey Street Gym and waited for it to open.

- END -

Acknowledgements

I'd like to thank the various people, places, and things responsible for the research, the writing and publishing of *The Favorite*.

First off, I'd like to thank the family and friends whose constant encouragement in the face of the insane endeavor of writing helped push me through goal after goal, and whose personalities constantly find their ways into my characters. There are too many to name specifically for fear of leaving someone out but you all know who you are. I would like to extend a special thanks to Dmitry Krugolets, a former co-worker of mine who imparted his passion for the sport and technical knowledge through hours of casual conversation and provided much insight through the early drafts.

I also want to thank my beta readers: Laura Paton, Michael Forrester, Ricky Hamilton, Chris and Jen Thomas, Sarah Miles, Tara Murracas, Jamie Bodnarchuk, Wolfgang Stufflebeam. I am so thankful to you for taking the time out of your busy day to help me. Special thanks to my editor, Michael Heatherly for being patient enough to help me fine-tune this. I also would like to thank Martin Gonzalez and his USMAA School in Bellingham, Washington, for allowing me to use their ring to brainstorm cover art.

Lastly, I'd like to thank all of you who read *The Fab 5*. You know who you are.